Praise for *Anecdotes*

"Part coming of age and part end times, *Anecdotes* is a bold and brilliant mixture of dark humour, understated literary experiments, and a poet's eye for the truth. Mockler's writing isn't afraid to look at the world and see it for what it is. Her stories are so deeply immersive you'll never want to leave. An absolute must-read if you live on this planet and even if you don't."
—Carleigh Baker, author of *Bad Endings*

"'What happened to you?' Terrible things do happen. Daily. From the opening story of a dead boy nobody loved, to anxiety-ridden days of overcrowded public buses and murderous job interviews, to birds dropping from the sky, to no one needing money anymore [or a stolen laptop] because the world is ending today and everyone still thinks it's happening to someone else while it's happening to them. Is it too late? Of course it is! 'What do they need?' Don't ask Pastor Rick. Like you, dear reader. 'They need to hold on real tight.' Mockler's *Anecdotes* is an instant 'post hope' classic!"
—Kirby, author of *Poetry is Queer*

"Utterly original, bracingly acidic, and always vulnerable, Kathryn Mockler channels Donald Barthelme having a psychotic break in this magnificent collection of coming-of-age stories for late stage capitalism."
—Emily Schultz, author of *The Blondes* and *Sleeping With Friends*

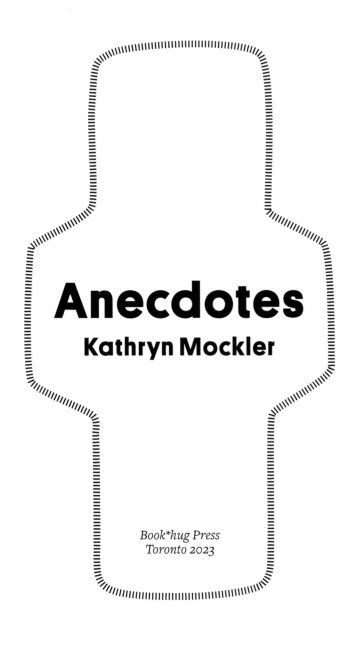

Anecdotes

Kathryn Mockler

*Book*hug Press*
Toronto 2023

First Edition

© 2023 by Kathryn Mockler

Library and Archives Canada Cataloguing in Publication

Title: Anecdotes / Kathryn Mockler.
Names: Mockler, Kathryn, 1971– author.
Identifiers: Canadiana (print) 20230220835 | Canadiana (ebook) 20230220843
  ISBN 9781771668446 (softcover)
  ISBN 9781771668453 (EPUB)
  ISBN 9781771668460 (PDF)
Subjects: LCGFT: Short stories.
Classification: LCC PS8626.O35 A83 2023 | DDC C813/.6—dc23

The production of this book was made possible through the generous assistance of the Canada Council for the Arts and the Ontario Arts Council. Book*hug Press also acknowledges the support of the Government of Canada through the Canada Book Fund and the Government of Ontario through the Ontario Book Publishing Tax Credit and the Ontario Book Fund.

Book*hug Press acknowledges that the land on which we operate is the traditional territory of many nations, including the Mississaugas of the Credit, the Anishnabeg, the Chippewa, the Haudenosaunee, and the Wendat peoples. We recognize the enduring presence of many diverse First Nations, Inuit, and Métis peoples and are grateful for the opportunity to meet and work on this territory.

CONTENTS

The Boy
Is Dead

THE BOY IS DEAD

The boy is dead, and we will spend the rest of the story trying to find out why and what happened and how it affected the people in the boy's life.

The boy came from a white middle-class family (his mother Protestant, his father Catholic) who were indifferent to him because he had a facial disfigurement from birth. As soon as he came into the world, he was not what they had anticipated. So they treated him more like a pet to keep fed and watered, which they did adequately.

While he is somewhat missed, his parents were able to get on with their lives fairly quickly after his death because they simply had not paid all that much attention to him when he was alive.

His parents had the boy because they thought it would strengthen their relationship, even though neither of them really had an interest in children. The boy had no siblings. His Catholic grandparents lived on the other side of the country and never got to know their grandchild. The boy's mother told him his grandparents took no interest in him because she refused to baptize him Catholic. His mother claimed she wanted the boy to make up his own idea about religion when he got older, but the boy knew the truth—she was ashamed to bring her disfigured child into the church.

Nonetheless, his Catholic grandparents sent him Christmas cards and modest birthday gifts. Once the boy's father took him to see his grandparents, but his father was really interested in visiting an ex-girlfriend, during a time that came to be known in the family as his mid-life crisis. The boy watched TV for the entire trip, and his grandmother cooked him frozen supermarket lasagna every night. Even her store-bought cookies tasted bad.

The boy felt unloved—although he never told anyone how he felt. Not even the school counsellor who was later arrested for sleeping with his students. In elementary school, during recess, the boy often hid in the bathroom so he wouldn't have to face being alone in the yard with all the other kids who had managed to form friends. The boy had often wondered how people formed friendships since he was pretty sure he didn't like a single person in his life and couldn't imagine voluntarily spending time with anyone. No, he did not play video games. No, he did not read. No, he was not creative and would never be great or one day appreciated. He was just a bored person who was terribly alone. He didn't like TV either but watched it because it gave him a good excuse to fix his eyes on something other than the ceiling.

His parents had threatened him with a psychologist, but he knew they would be too preoccupied with themselves and their own problems—their affairs, their jobs that they hated, their worries about money—to do anything about it. When his mother said "psychologist," the boy would nod and put his arm over his eyes. They wouldn't take him to an appointment, and even if they set one up, he wouldn't go.

The boy's father hated fat people. Every night at the dinner table, he would talk about the woman he worked with. He called her fat and a loudmouth and a busybody. The boy thought his father didn't like the woman because she reminded the boy's father of his mother (the boy's grandmother).

When the police found the boy's body in the river—bloated and decomposed, almost unrecognizable, the boy's parents hadn't even known he was missing and couldn't remember the name of his dentist. Oh sure, his mother cried when she realized she wouldn't be someone's mother anymore, but she wasn't affected in a really significant way. She had liked the idea of being someone's mother—just not this boy's mother. She felt a sort of relief upon hearing about his death, like when you are fired from a job you hate but still need the money. There's that twinge of regret and wondering if you did everything you could to keep the job, but then the next morning you wake and realize this was the best thing that could have ever happened to you. The boy's mother felt like a reset button had been pushed on her life that said: *Start Now*.

To ease her heavy burden of having to be the boy's mother when he was alive, his mother had taken to drinking vodka every night. The boy's father left when he was five, and from that time on, the boy and his mother ate their dinners in separate rooms. His mother sat in her yellow chair in the living room and the boy sat on the couch in the den. The two rooms were attached, with the TV in the middle. They could watch the same program without actually having to sit in the same room and face each other. They did this night after night, hardly speaking, watching game show after game show until his mother passed out and the boy put her to bed.

After the boy's father left, there was a string of babysitters. On three occasions, the boy was molested. He told no one. He felt ashamed. He felt it was his fault. The molesters knew that such a shy and withdrawn and disfigured kid would tell no one. He was the perfect target. And they were right.

The boy's childhood was spent avoiding people. Once he got into high school, he focused on his classes. He wasn't particularly smart and didn't get good grades, but he always did his homework because it was a decent way to pass the time. He could have taken up smoking but didn't because the smell reminded him of the smell of his mother.

The boy had a death wish but wasn't in danger of killing

himself, because he feared pain. He feared directing pain at himself but wasn't particularly afraid if pain happened to him or if the pain took him by surprise. Once he accidentally smashed his arm through a glass door and didn't feel the pain because his arm went numb. He didn't even know he was cut until he saw the blood. Instead of harming himself, the boy found compromising situations to insert himself in, hoping something would happen to him that would accidentally render him unconscious or dead.

With his death wish in mind, the boy set out to the secluded part of the park on a Wednesday in the spring in hopes that he could attract a creep who might take him away in a car. What he found instead were trees and chipmunks and a couple making out by the stream. "None of this makes sense," the boy said to himself. "Why do some people get lucky while others have such a hard time?" The boy didn't care about the other people who had a hard time. He only cared about the hard time he was having. He walked away from the couple and sat by himself on the swing. A small child asked the boy to push him, and the boy said no and walked away so he could be by himself with his thoughts.

You might be disappointed to know that the boy was not in fact murdered. He actually tripped on a tree root, hit his head on a stone, and fell into the river, where he drowned because no one saw him. Since his parents had not reported him missing, no one was looking for him. Everyone just went on as they always had. The boy lay in the river for days because the weather had been bad and no one was walking along the trail, or if they were, they hadn't bothered to look at the river in the particular spot where the boy had lain. Someone might have ridden by on a bike, but they would have been going too fast to see the boy's body in the water.

We're not to feel sad for the boy because he would have

rathered be dead than alive. He didn't feel pain as his head hit the rock. It was like the glass door—he was in a state of shock and then everything went black. He didn't even have time to scream. But had he had time to utter a sound, it would have been the word *now*.

I wrote this story about a boy in the hope that you would find it more interesting than if it had been written about a girl with the same experiences. Really, this is a story about my family and me. Many details have been changed, but most of it is true.

HUMAN MICROPHONE

1.

The other day, I was on a bus that stopped in front of a school and a stream of middle-school-age children boarded.

I'm claustrophobic, so I decided this would be a sign for me to get off immediately and walk home.

When I got to the back door, it was locked.

As more children boarded the bus, I called out to the driver, "Could you please open the door?" But my voice was drowned out by the laughs and chatter of the excited children who were packing themselves into the bus and swarming all around me.

It was a Friday, and the frenzy of the weekend was in the air.

A kid standing nearby heard me and called out in a booming pubescent voice: "Open the door!"

Then, in a chain reaction, more students chanted, "Open the door! Open the door! Open the door! Open the door! Open the door! Open the door! Open the door!"

Their voices increased in volume and formed a human microphone, with their shouts moving quickly from the back to the front of the bus.

But the driver ignored them.

In the next moment, it was like the children were reading my thoughts and saying them out loud to one another.

One said to her friend, "Why won't he open the door?"

Another said, "He's not going to open the door."

A third said, "What's she going to do?"

What *was* I going to do? Well, I was having a panic attack for one thing and needed to get off the bus immediately. A therapist once told me that anxiety often arises when we overestimate our danger and underestimate our ability to cope, which was the exact situation I found myself in. But you can't reason with fear, and this was vying to be my worst panic attack yet.

I shook the door again, and still it wouldn't budge.

A man standing next to me said, "He'll open the door once all the children have boarded."

"Oh, I see," I said, smiling sheepishly. "I guess I started something."

He did not smile back. "You did," he said.

As more children boarded the bus, there was less room to move or breathe, and my panic really set in. No amount of mindfulness or breathing or positive self-talk would get me out of this. On a scale of one to ten, this was one hundred. I knew it, the children knew it, but the bus driver did not.

Even though it was clear that the door was locked, I shook the handles desperately. And when the children saw my desperation, they once again formed a human microphone.

This time their calls were louder and angrier and had a greater sense of outrage and urgency.

They were serious in their attempts to get the bus driver's attention, but also they must have delighted in the fact that they were able to scream so loudly and with such demand at an adult on behalf of another adult.

"Open the door!" they screamed over and over. "Open the door!" Never have I had anyone in my corner like those kids on that bus.

The bus driver said nothing.

Once the bus was completely packed so that none of us could move, the driver finally opened the back door, and I tumbled out onto the sidewalk, gasping for air.

"Have a nice day, ma'am," said one of the most vocal kids, waving as the bus pulled away.

2.

The next day I was at a department store downtown, and the sales clerk would not take back a red sweater I had bought. She claimed the item was final sale even though it did not say final sale on my receipt.

Immediately after I'd bought it, I regretted the decision. I can take it back, I told myself, and thought I'd see how it looked in my own mirror at home. I thought if I tried it on with the right shoes or the right skirt, the sweater would suit me.

It didn't.

To make matters worse, the sweater was way out of my price range. I paid nearly three hundred dollars for this name-brand sweater. I'd never done such a thing before, and I wasn't sure what had come over me. In the moment before I bought the sweater, I had wanted it more than I wanted anything else on earth. The urge was so powerful and desperate, I would have done anything to own this item of clothing.

Even though I knew this sweater was out of my price range and would eat up the small amount of credit I had left on my credit card, I clung to the fact that I could return it within thirty days.

I'd meant to go back to the department store the next day but found out that my mother had a gambling addiction and had gotten into a serious amount of debt. I was so preoccupied with what the next few months would look like that I forgot about the sweater and how much I'd paid for it and how much I did not like it, no matter the lighting, no matter the style of my shoe.

It wasn't until I was straightening up my bedroom that I came across the department store bag under a pile of dirty clothes. My stomach lurched. I checked the receipt and discovered, much to my relief, that this was the last day I could return it. I cancelled all my morning appointments and set off for the department store.

"The receipt says I have thirty days to return it," I said. "Today is the thirtieth day."

The sales clerk looked at it and then examined the sweater more carefully. She was a middle-aged woman who looked younger than her years, owing to her short stylish hair and purple highlights. "Well, I'm afraid I can't return it because it has been worn."

"I never wore it," I said. "It's been sitting in this bag for the last thirty days."

The woman shook her head.

"How could I have worn the sweater if it didn't even fit?" I pointed out that the tags were still attached to the sweater.

"Anyone can wear clothes with sales tags and anyone can wear clothes that don't fit," she said. "Look at that woman over there with the coat that's too big."

I turned to look at the woman who was swimming in a pea coat.

"And that man with the short pants." She pointed at the sweater angrily. "Your sweater has all the telltale signs of being worn. The wool is balled up, the arms are stretched out, and it smells like you," she said. "You cannot deny that it smells like you."

Behind me were frustrated customers who wanted this dispute to be settled so they could pay for their items and go home or to the movies or out for dinner or for a walk along a friendly beach.

I could hear someone behind me sigh, and I imagined the others looking at their phones or rolling their eyes. I knew what it felt like to be in line behind a customer with a dispute. However, I had paid a great deal of money for this sweater, and I wasn't willing to back down so easily, although I have to admit my face was burning.

I generally don't like to cause a fuss or bother people who are just trying to do their job. I will rarely, if ever, send back food in a restaurant or complain to a manager about bad service. But this sweater cost three hundred dollars.

Even though she needed to get back to her increasingly impatient customers, the sales clerk folded up the sweater with the utmost care, as if it were an item I wanted instead of something I was trying to unload. Then she placed it back in the department store bag.

"Perhaps you can take it to a consignment store," she said, and handed the bag back to me. "Next," she called to the customer behind me and turned away, shutting me out of her world completely.

As the customer approached the counter, I didn't move. I was stunned. I looked down at the sweater and couldn't stop thinking about the three hundred dollars I had basically just dumped into the garbage. Was this how my mother felt when she went to the casino? The sinking feeling of having done something that you just couldn't take back?

I stood at the counter while the sales clerk rung up the man's purchases. They both pretended I wasn't there.

I looked at her, but she wouldn't look at me.

As I was about to take my bag and head home, I heard the cries and laughs of the schoolchildren from the bus. At first their sounds were faint, but as they neared the sales desk, their voices grew louder.

The children began to appear from behind clothing racks and mannequin displays. They poured out of elevators and slid down escalator rails. They teemed from change rooms and popped up from under tables.

The sales clerk, and the other customers, for that matter, seemed oblivious.

The children were at the age where they were starting to flirt and compete with one another. As they made their way toward me, there was pushing and shoving and bra snapping and tripping. Their pimply faces had broad smiles and their crooked teeth were braced or retained. The odour of sweat and hormones filled the air.

They gathered around me and chanted to the sales clerk: "Take it back. Take it back. Take it back."

The children's voices were in unison, as if they had practised saying these words for weeks or even years. Their timing was impeccable, their projection loud and clear.

Their voices filled up the store the way the sound of a choir fills up a music hall. It was beautiful and heartbreaking and deeply moving.

The sales clerk picked up the phone by her register and spoke into it and then listened to someone on the other end. The children were so loud I could not tell if she was really talking to someone or just faking it.

And then, without a word, she issued my refund. She pointed to the back of the receipt where I had to write my name, phone number, address, and the reason for the return. It could have all been so easy if she hadn't created a problem where there was no problem.

She took my receipt, then handed me the cash, which, bolstered by the children's chanting, I counted in front of her slowly and deliberately. All three hundred dollars and fifty-eight cents. Then I nodded and left the store, escorted by the children.

When we reached the street, the children faded into the crowd like a helpful stranger who hands you a scarf or a glove you've absent-mindedly dropped and disappears before you can thank them.

3.

I've learned to get my elderly cat to pee on demand. Sometimes he complains about it with a grumpy meow, but most of the time he heads straight to the litter box when I say, "Pee-pee."

It's not a trick; it came out of an episode when he didn't pee for nearly two days and had to see the vet for a catheter. I don't ever want to go through such an ordeal again, plus it cost three thousand dollars.

All this to say I cannot summon the children on demand even though I can make my cat pee.

For instance, the other day I was on my way to an environmental protest in the park, passing through an alley, when I had a conflict with a woman I'd witnessed hitting her dog.

It was a little dog and she screamed and yelled at it and hit it several times. Then she picked it up and walked out of the alley and onto the street. Without seeing her hit the dog, you would have thought her just some nice lady with a dog. She was well dressed and looked like the type of woman who owned a successful business and went on expensive luxury vacations with her best girlfriends where they would drink elaborate cocktails named after 1940s starlets.

I couldn't figure out what the dog had done to elicit such a response. It wasn't even a yappy, ugly dog. It was one of those dogs that had cute, sad-looking eyes.

As the woman and the dog walked away, I burned with anger. Without thinking, I followed the woman into the small market.

I told her I'd witnessed her hitting her dog, and she told me to mind my own business.

"You made it my business when you hit your dog in public." Then I said, "You shouldn't have a dog if you can't take care of it."

Much to my surprise she said, "You're right," and handed me the dog.

At that point, I wasn't sure what to do. She had acquiesced so completely there had hardly even been a conflict.

Perhaps that's why the children didn't come.

I looked around, expecting the children to surface, but they were nowhere to be seen. I was on my own and couldn't think of what to say or do. My mind went blank. The owner of the store frowned at me, likely for having a dog inside.

The woman who had handed me her dog picked up her shopping cart and began to shop for vegetables as if nothing had transpired.

I followed behind her, holding the dog. He was cute and sort of cuddled into me like a sweet baby.

The woman did not speak to me, and I did not speak to her. I just followed as she picked up and put down items and occasionally placed them in her cart. She picked up apples and checked to make sure they were firm. She chose pasta and green beans and luncheon meat and lettuce and then a bag of chips and some frozen dinners. It all looked very appealing, even though it was nothing I would purchase for myself. I imagined eating a nice sandwich and some potato chips. I was hungry because I had skipped lunch so I wouldn't be late for the protest.

As we made our way through the store, the dog started whining and whimpering. It was an upsetting sound. I tried to pet the dog and bounce the dog but nothing would stop him from crying.

"What do I do?" I asked her.

"He needs to go out for a walk," she said with the same sharp judgment I had recently bestowed on her. The tables were turning. "He needs to go pee," she said.

I put the dog down and held his leash. "What's his name?" I asked.

"I never gave him one." She picked up some on-sale spinach and made her way to the cash register.

I took the dog outside.

The woman was right, he did need to pee and peed as soon

as we got out of the store and then went back to his friendly disposition.

I looked at my watch. I felt slightly guilty about skipping the protest. But it wasn't fair to bring the dog to a protest that would attract thousands, so we walked home in the rain.

4.

"She never even gave him a name," I said to my husband, who was eating leftover pizza for dinner.

"We can't keep him. He's not our dog."

"I think he actually is our dog," I said. "She gave him to me."

"You can't just give a stranger a dog on the street."

"She was hitting him, so I don't think she wanted him anymore. It seemed like the dog was too much for her. Once she gave him up, it was a relief. Her disposition was more pleasant—almost someone I could have been friends with in another life if she hadn't met me as a stranger who accosted her on the street.

"She responded to my conflict with immediate withdrawal. No fighting. No defending herself or denying that she had been wrong. She just agreed with me and gave me the dog. It was like she had been waiting for me to come along and take the dog off her hands, and I had been waiting to receive it."

"Yes," my husband said, "but now we have a dog we don't want."

"I want him," I said. "And I'm going to keep him."

"First of all, what about the cat?" he asked. "The cat will not like the dog."

"He'll have to get used to it."

"The cat has an anxiety disorder. We can't keep him in a state of constant anxiety or he'll start peeing blood again," my husband reasoned.

"Maybe he'll like the dog," I offered. "We should at least give it a try."

"You need to take the dog to a shelter."

"I'm going to tell you one thing," I said, imagining the group of children all around me cheering me on, coming to my defence, and shouting, *Let her keep the dog.* "I'm going to win this fight."

"Okay," my husband said, immediately backing down.

"Okay?" I asked.

"Yeah, okay," he said. "We can keep the dog."

That night I slept better than I had in years.

I dreamed I searched for the children high and low in mountains and towns, in kitchen cupboards, and in crawl spaces. Whenever I got close to finding them, they always slipped just out of reach.

DARK THOUGHTS

In the park, a dude abruptly says to his two old-timey hippie friends, "I'm not into postmodernism and all that garbage."

One hippie says, "I'm not into parks."

The park says, "I'm not into dudes or hippies or squirrels or unhappy parents who scream at their children to stay clear of the road so they don't get run over by a bike or SUV."

"What would happen if I didn't tell them to stop running?" one parent thinks to herself and shares with no one until her next psychotherapy appointment. The thought causes her a great deal of distress. To relieve herself of the guilt, she treats her children to ice cream and fries from the food truck across from the park, but she won't let anyone enjoy the food. She tells them what they are eating will clog their arteries. She tells them about carbs and bad fats and the new diet she's on and all the weight she's lost. She wants everyone to feel as bad about themselves as she does about herself.

The park says, "If I have to see one more lover kiss another lover on the shoulder, something drastic will happen."

THE JOB INTERVIEW: A MURDER

I had always been a careful person. Neurotic, in fact. I wouldn't walk at night alone. Ever. I always double-checked that the doors were locked before bed. I touched the burners on the stove more times than I cared to admit before I left the house. I wouldn't mix Tylenol and alcohol because it could harm my liver. I read the directions on all my medications. Rarely would I jaywalk. I basically lived my life thinking the worst possible thing was going to happen at any moment, and I did my best to prevent it. The methods of operating my life in this way were the result of obsessive compulsions, a hypochondriacal mother, and the fact that we live in a nightmare with no plausible explanation for how or why we are here.

My husband and I had been living in Windsor, Ontario, for about a year so he could attend a graduate program in visual arts. I had graduated from my master's program in creative writing the previous year, after which I was fortunate enough to get a grant to write a book of poetry. But the money was now running out, and I needed a job badly.

There were at least two reasons I always had trouble getting jobs. I suffered from extreme underconfidence and I had terrible anxiety, making job interviews nearly impossible. I couldn't relax. I couldn't be myself, and so I immediately turned off potential employers—understandably so.

Because I was a student for years and hadn't required the type of clothing needed for a professional job, I didn't have much in the way of a wardrobe. I wore casual clothes around the house and I had my one outfit that I liked to wear when we went out. One night when we were at an art opening, a woman from my husband's program who I did not particularly like turned to me in front of a group of people and said, "Do you only have that one outfit? Is that like your uniform? Because every time I see you, you're wearing the same thing."

I don't know how, but I managed to stammer an attempt at self-mockery. "Yes, it's my uniform. It's the only thing I like to wear."

Then I quickly excused myself to the bathroom and sobbed. Big wet sloppy tears poured out of my eyes. I could hear people chatting and laughing on the other side of the door. I cried like a kid who had just been picked on by a schoolyard bully—even though I was twenty-eight years old. I felt shame and hatred and anger all at once. All my good comeback lines played themselves over and over in my head.

Yes, I really did only have that one outfit. It served as both my job interview outfit and my going-out outfit—a black blazer, a light-blue collared shirt with blue flowers, and black pants. It was the only outfit I felt good in since I had recently gained some weight.

So here I was in Windsor, Ontario, looking for a job, a little more desperate than usual since the "uniform" comment. The problem for me in terms of getting a job, in addition to my confidence and anxiety issues, was that I had no skills. I wasn't experienced enough to get a teaching job, and the jobs I had held in the past—house cleaning, dishwashing, and factory work—I didn't particularly want. I was too terrified of people to waitress and too terrified of cash registers to work as a cashier.

I had always longed to work in a bookstore or a library, but I could never land one of those coveted positions. So that pretty much left me applying for administrative work, which was also proving impossible to get in this small, economically depressed town.

I applied to several temp agencies and took all their demoralizing personality, word processing, and Excel spreadsheet tests, and I looked in the paper every day to see if there were any listings for odd jobs. For a little while, things were starting to look up. I got one day of temp work answering phones at a paper factory, and I made it to the second-round interview stage at the Nutrition Hut in the mall, but, ultimately, they turned me down, claiming I wasn't experienced enough.

So I continued to scan newspaper ads until I found one from a company looking for part-time admin help for a small family-run business. They were going to pay ten dollars an hour, which was better than minimum wage.

I called the number right away and set up an appointment.

Even though I put on the "uniform" and told my husband I was going to an interview before I left the apartment, I realized, as I got off the bus and walked down what looked like a residential street in an older subdivision, I had not given him the address or phone number. That was kind of a stupid thing to do, I thought to myself as I stood in front of the house.

I considered just walking away, but there were a couple of kids playing out front: a little boy with a skateboard and a little girl wearing a pink dress and heavy black shoes, which made the place seem safe enough, so I decided to knock on the door.

A guy with a moustache, wearing cut-offs and an undershirt, answered in bare feet. If this was a story, I thought to myself with a little laugh, he'd be a cliché.

Since I'd started writing, a little game I played with myself was picking out people who I thought were clichés. The boy was a little-boy cliché and his sister would have been a little-girl cliché if she hadn't been wearing such unusual shoes. As I straightened my black blazer and adjusted my blue-flower shirt, I thought about the woman who had insulted me at the art opening and decided she was a grad school cliché. And although I didn't know it at the time, I too would become a cliché—a dead-girl cliché.

The boy from the front yard ran up to the door and said, "Hi, John, can I come over and play video games?"

"Not right now, Ethan. We've got a guest," he said, and let me inside.

I took off my shoes and looked around. The place seemed normalish enough, a little messy but nothing really out of the ordinary except that all the furniture was white.

John said, "Our office is downstairs," and he led me all the way to the back of the house. The house was long. It seemed to take forever to get from one end to the other.

As we walked through the living room and then dining room and then to a little porch, the two kids from outside followed us along the side of the house. They banged on the windows and yelled things at us, and by the time we got to the back, Ethan and his sister were standing at the screen door.

"Who is the blond lady?" Ethan asked. "Is she the same one from before?"

"None of your beeswax," John said. He had this strange ability to be nice to the kid and mean to the kid at the same time.

"Can we come in, John?" Ethan asked.

"Not now," the man said. "Go home." And he shut the door in the little boy's grinning stupid face.

God, that kid is annoying, I thought.

"John," Ethan pleaded. "I don't want to go home."

I do, I thought. I want to go home right now.

"Get outta here," John said, this time with a firmer tone.

There's a weird, prickly feeling you get when you realize you could be in serious danger.

Some people call it a sixth sense or intuition. I remember a guest on *Oprah* talking about self-defence and how women can sense danger before they are actually in danger. It's kind of like built-in radar, a protection device. It's something you should always listen to, she said. It's something you should never ignore because it could save your life. When you get these sensations, your body is trying to tell you something.

She was right. I had this radar. And I knew I had it. I knew I had it because when I took one look at the outside of the house, the feeling was there—that sense or instinct that told me I might be headed for danger. A voice inside my head said, *It's not worth it—go home.* And as I was stepping inside the door, that same voice tried to stop me. I knew I shouldn't have gone in, but I went in anyway because I wanted to believe there was a job that would pay me ten dollars an hour. I won't eat mayonnaise past the expiration date, and yet somehow I managed to find myself in a strange man's basement and no one knew I was there.

Before we went downstairs, John told me to put on some slippers because the basement floor was dirty.

Along the edge of the back porch, several house slippers of different sizes were lined up in a neat row. The slippers were blackened with dirt and they smelled, and even though I declined them at first, John insisted.

"We don't want your sock feet to get dirty," he said, and there was a tone in his voice that made me feel like I couldn't refuse.

So I picked the least offensive pair and put them on, trying my best not to show my disgust as I walked down the rickety steps to a newly renovated basement that smelled like Ikea furniture, cigarette smoke, and black mould.

Another man was sitting at a round table near a kitchenette smoking. He too had a moustache. And he too looked like a cliché. He looked like a cliché of a man who might cause me harm. On the table beside him, a forty-ounce bottle of rye and a shot glass.

This wasn't a job interview. There was no family business.

"Would you like a drink," the man said. It was a statement rather than a question, and like with the slippers, I couldn't refuse.

The job ad had been a ruse. No one pays over minimum wage if they don't have to.

I thought about Ethan, who in one moment I found as annoying as a persistent housefly and in the next my lifeline. I prayed he wouldn't give up trying to play video games with John. Maybe he would break in. Maybe he would tell his mother that something terrible was taking place.

But in the end little Ethan couldn't do anything to save me. In his last attempt to get inside, he banged on the basement window and waved with a dazed and wild smile on his face. To be honest, he looked more like a maniac than any of them. Maybe he wasn't a cliché after all. But John just ignored the kid and pulled down the blinds.

"I like your shirt, lady," Ethan said through the window.

Then I heard Ethan hop on his skateboard and ride down the gravel driveway, his sister clomping after him in her heavy shoes. I wondered if Ethan would tell someone that I had been there, that he had seen me? Would his sister? Were they too young to remember or would they even care?

LET'S PLAY OIL SLICK

Two children are playing together in a schoolyard.

A: Let's play oil slick.
B: I get to be the bird, and you can be the rescuer.
A: I want to be the bird. Now wash my hair.
B: You wash *my* hair. You were the bird last time.
A: I'm not playing unless I get to play the character I want.
B: Why don't you be the bird, and I'll be the sea otter.
A: Who will rescue us?
B: Nobody.

IT'S ANTICIPATION THAT'S KEEPING ME ALIVE

If you're cold, take off your sweater and come inside. And if you need a drink, get it yourself from the beer fridge. I'm not the host. I'm just sitting here waiting to see what's going to happen next. It's exciting, even if on the surface everything looks ordinary. The waterglasses next to the table. The throw pillows on the green couch.

The wind rustling the leaves in the trees while someone throws a lit cigarette into the street. In a moment, it might rain or maybe not. But it doesn't matter because it's anticipation that's keeping me alive.

Yesterday a snail crossed my path on the sidewalk. I picked her up and put her in the garden, so she wouldn't get crushed by my foot when she hadn't even made it to the halfway mark of her journey.

The snail's plight wasn't any of my business, but I have a saviour complex. I don't think she appreciated my intervention, because she crawled into her house and didn't come out.

Where are you in your journey?

And what would make you retreat into your shell?

I'm in the blue void. But something will happen eventually. I just know it.

COOKIES

—I have become a person who brushes her cat's teeth.

—Everyone has to start somewhere.

—Where are you off to?

—Book club. You?

—I have an appointment with a dentist who tells bad jokes and talks about politics while his hands are in my mouth, so I can't talk back.

—That sounds like the dentist I went to see last week. Were you spying on me?

—No, I was sleeping.

—Prove it.

—I dreamed a woman was trying to hit me with a long stick in the attic of a mansion in a small town. Outside, the grass was wet and green. People walked in the yard in black rubber boots so they didn't get their feet wet. They never left the grounds and walked in circles in groups of three and complained about the weather. Someone nearby was baking cookies but never offered any. I don't like sweets, but I would have enjoyed the opportunity to refuse the invitation for a reason I made up on the spot.

—Did she hit you?

—Who?

—The women with the stick.

—No, she missed.

WALKING

I'll walk with my head down because I hate myself, and you'll walk with your eyes on your phone because you hate everyone else, and maybe we'll crash into each other on the sidewalk.

WHEN A TREE DEVELOPS PROBLEMS

Let's be vague. Instead of talking, let's perform our favourite emojis for the crowd. Don't worry, no one is watching. No one cares what we say or do unless we take a picture of ourselves in a mirror and put it on the internet.

I'll be a wilted flower, and you can be a tree.

Pick any kind of tree, but make sure it is a desirable species. The tree must have a disease, which will require it to be taken down by the city, despite the protests.

The neighbour you thought you liked will want the tree destroyed because the roots interfere with the pipes in the sewer system.

The neighbour you've always despised will want to save the tree because it provides a nice shade over their swimming pool in summer. This will surprise you, and you will not know whose side to take.

If the tree is already dead, let it be hollow, and let it be located under a power line.

Should there be a lightning storm, let the tree and whatever is near be electrocuted.

Sure, that woman who lives two blocks over will chain herself to the tree because that's the way it goes, but eventually she'll get tired and hungry and will want to go home.

This doesn't have to be sad story.

YOU KNOW WHAT'S GREAT?

Two friends are sitting in a coffee shop, drinking hot drinks.

A: The world is a terrible place. But you know what's *great* about it?

B: What?

A: (*Smiling*) I don't care anymore!

B: (*Frowning*) Don't you think you're being selfish? Don't you think you're being rude?

A: No. I think I'm being just like everybody else.

B: Is it wise to be like everyone else?

A: Yes. Instead of getting worked up and losing sleep, I'm watching events unfold like I'm in a movie theatre but sitting far away from the front row.

B: Can you order popcorn?

A: I can order all the popcorn I want and some red licorice. And you know what?

B: What?

A: The seats are very comfortable and no one blocks my view—not even the man with the oversized head who claims to know how the film will end.

B: Does the film make anyone cry?

A: No. No one is crying.

B: Why not? Isn't it a sad story?

A: Yes, it is a very sad story because everyone still thinks it's happening to someone else while it's happening to them.

WHITECAPS

If I tell you that the universe is a cat, you probably won't believe me. You'll say, "There you go making up stories again."

I'll say, "I guess you have to be there to understand." I know, it sounds condescending and, at the same time, like I'm a religious fanatic.

"Why then," you'll ask, "if the universe is a cat, do we see the moon in daylight?"

I'll say something I read off a blog post like, "Sometimes the moon is the closest object to Earth and sometimes it is brighter in the day than at night."

You'll be impressed but request to see the instructional video. Then you'll say, "All this space talk is making me want a peanut butter sandwich," and I'll agree because I'm actually feeling kind of hungry.

We will arrange to talk about the weather and how bad the storm was last night and how the wind shook the windowpanes and kept Grandma awake into the wee hours. We'll talk about how the wind still feels cool against my cheek and how the waves have whitecaps on them.

You'll ask, "What are whitecaps?"

And I'll say, "Whitecaps are a sign that anyone can drown if they want or if they aren't taking precautions. For instance, don't go out in a canoe in this kind of weather, especially if you aren't a strong swimmer and have memories of the swimming instructor calling you a baby while you cried and shivered at the side of the pool, because the boat will surely tip and there's no lifeguard on shore."

At this point we will decide to leave the matters of the universe to others and try as best we can to get on with what we have come to accept as our meaningless, trite, and petty lives, until we arrive safely in the next world.

THE VISION

Rowan started gambling at the airport. Sasha and Tony had each lost twenty dollars and stood behind Rowan as she proceeded to drop five hundred on her credit card.

"This is dangerous," she said, laughing.

"You're going to lose all your money," Sasha said. "We haven't even got to the hotel."

Rowan used the arm on the slot machine even though she could have pressed the button. "It makes me feel like I'm doing something," she said.

"You're not doing anything but losing money," Sasha said.

"I'm going for cigarettes," Tony said.

"We're on a strict gambling budget," Sasha said. "You should have one."

After the entire five hundred was spent, Sasha and Tony got Rowan to relinquish her slot machine. As they walked toward the cab stand, Rowan looked back at it sadly.

"You're a born gambler," Sasha said. "You better watch out or this trip could ruin you."

"Hotel Excalibur," Tony told the cab driver.

"We're going to find other things to do here besides gambling," Sasha scolded. She was holding a brochure. "We're going to eat in nice restaurants. We're going to sightsee. We're going to go to shows and go shopping. We are not spending all our time in the casino."

Rowan didn't hear any of it. Her head was resting against the passenger window, and she was fast asleep.

Hotel Excalibur was a cartoon-like white castle, moated, situated beside the Luxor Hotel. When they walked into the lobby, large signs advertised a jousting match called the Tournament of Kings, a nightly dinner show that was the hotel's main attraction. Hotel Excalibur catered to families. There were gift shops filled with King Arthur and Merlin figurines and a video arcade with retro video games and pinball machines.

"I thought the whole place would be a lot classier," Rowan said to Tony. "You know, showgirls and guys dressed in snazzy suits."

"That's Las Vegas of another era," Sasha said.

"This place looks like an amusement park," Tony said, looking at the long line of tourists in shorts waiting to be seated for the buffet.

They went to their rooms to change and freshen up.

Rowan turned on the TV and set her suitcase on the bed. The room smelled of flowers and vanilla, and it caught Rowan at the back of her throat and made her cough.

She looked around for the source of the smell and found a plug-in air freshener, which she removed and set on the night table. In the bathroom mirror she saw bags under her eyes. She saw her greying hair.

Because the room was cold from air conditioning, Rowan ran a hot shower and the bathroom filled with steam. She showered and dried herself with a towel while worrying about what she would wear. She had only brought jeans and two black suits. She hadn't even packed enough underwear for the trip. She put on a white shirt and one of the suits and looked more like she was ready for a business meeting than a vacation.

Rowan coughed and knocked on Tony and Sasha's door. Tony opened it. He had a beer in his hand.

"Where did you get that?" Rowan asked.

"From the mini-bar."

"It's going to cost you a fortune," Rowan said.

"Don't you look fancy," Sasha said with a hint of criticism.

Tony was wearing jeans and Sasha was wearing shorts and a T-shirt.

"This is all I brought," Rowan said.

Sasha put her purse over her shoulder, and they walked to the elevator.

The elevator was mirrored, and Rowan looked at herself in the reflection. "All the things you look forward to end up being a disappointment."

"You sound like someone in a mid-life crisis," Sasha said, rubbing Rowan's back.

"Or maybe I just get my hopes too high," Rowan said. "Maybe if I had lower expectations."

"Have you thought of antidepressants?" Sasha asked.

"Let's go to the casino," Tony suggested.

Rowan sat at a dollar slot machine, and Tony and Sasha sat on either side of her. Rowan's initial enthusiasm for gambling was now gone. She looked at the people around her. "Everyone is really depressing," she said.

"So, so what? Worry about yourself." Tony put five dollars in his slot machine.

Sasha won eighty bucks. Tony and Rowan looked over at her with interest.

"I'm gonna cash out," Sasha said as the coins dropped into the trough.

"You've got to play your winnings," Tony said.

"Then you never win," Rowan said.

"No, that's how you win big," he said.

"That's how you lose everything." Sasha took her money from the machine. "I'm going buy us all drinks."

"Drinks are complementary," Tony said. "Look." He pointed to the server coming around with a tray. "You just have to tip."

"It's so people keep throwing money at these machines,"

Rowan said, pushing the button. She'd given up on the arm. Something about Sasha winning that money gave Rowan a sinking feeling.

"Don't be so bleak, honey," Sasha said. "You're just going through a rough time. Things will pick up."

* * *

At four o'clock in the afternoon, Tony declared he was hungry. They stood in front of the Tournament of Kings entrance and read a sign warning that the jousting dinner was not suitable for people with asthma.

"We'll go someplace else," Sasha said.

"No," Rowan said. "I want you two to go. This is your vacation too. You don't need to babysit me."

Sasha looked at Tony, unsure.

"We'll meet up for drinks later," Tony said.

"We can't leave her," Sasha said as Rowan walked away from them and out the front door of the hotel.

Rowan made her way along Las Vegas Boulevard. The heat was relentless and hit the back of her head in a throbbing ache. She passed tourist families and wedding parties and couples. There was a just-married couple in their twenties walking down the strip. He wore a black suit and she a black evening dress. His hair was prematurely greying, and her hair was dyed blond. She held a yellow bouquet. They were beaming in a way that indicated strangers should congratulate them, which they did. Something about them bugged Rowan and made her want to say, "It won't last" or "Get out while you still can."

But she did not. Instead she walked into an old hotel and put twenty dollars into a slot machine, lost it all in minutes, then left.

Rowan saw a car rental agency and went inside. "I'd like to rent a car," she said to the clerk, who was on the phone.

"For how long?" the clerk asked.

"I don't know," Rowan said.

"It's cheaper if you rent for three days."

"Okay," she said.

The clerk completed the paperwork.

Rowan leaned over the counter to see what the clerk was doing.

"You're Canadian," the clerk sad.

"Yes," Rowan said.

"Me too. I'm from Winnipeg. Couldn't take the winters so I moved to one of the hottest places on earth!" she laughed.

Rowan knew the clerk was only trying to be friendly but couldn't stand the sound of the woman's voice.

The car she rented was a small sedan. She got in, threw away the pine air freshener, then she drove out of the city and into the surrounding desert.

On the highway it was sunset, and the sun was strong. She could hardly see the road for the black spots that appeared in front of her eyes. Her eyeballs hurt and the back of her head still throbbed. She turned on the radio and a country song played.

The sky was blue with light clouds. An airplane flew above. She pulled out her cellphone and speed-dialled a number.

"Oliver," Rowan said. "It's Mommy."

"Hi, Mommy. Did you go on a plane?"

"Yes."

"Was it a big plane?" Oliver asked.

"Yes."

"How big?"

"Very big."

"Can I go with you next time?"

"Maybe," Rowan said. Her eyes filled with tears and her throat hurt, knowing she would not be seeing him any time soon.

Manny got on the phone. "Why are you calling here?"

"I wanted to say hi to my son," Rowan said.

"You can't call here whenever you feel like it. We have plans."

"I'm sorry," Rowan said.

"Say goodbye to your mother," Manny said.

"Goodbye, Mommy."

Rowan threw the phone on the passenger seat beside her. With her sun visor down, she stared at the mountains ahead of her, at the lines on the road, at a red car directly in front her with a bumper sticker that read *Support Our Troops*.

And when the road curved and the sun came in through a part of the window the visor couldn't protect, Rowan looked at the road as long as she could stand it, then looked away.

She repeated this until the sun lowered and no longer hurt her eyes.

The radio had turned to static, and Rowan, preoccupied with driving, had not changed the station.

The red car ahead seemed to slow down, so Rowan passed it. With the red car in the distance, she was alone on the road now.

Everything was empty and quiet in the few moments between day and night. And that's when the vision appeared to Rowan. It was terrifying and thrilling at the same time. Specific and vague. She knew everything that is, was, and would ever be—all at the same time.

Rowan had no idea how long the vision lasted. It could have been moments. It could have been days. When it was over, Rowan lost control of the car, and it flipped but landed upright at the side of the road.

Unharmed, she stared ahead, panting. The red car had finally caught up to Rowan and stopped.

The driver got out and knocked on her window. "Are you okay?" he asked.

Rowan turned to him. She was speechless.

"Do you want me to call someone?"

Rowan shook her head.

"Do you need a doctor?"

Rowan shook her head again.

"Does your car work?"

"I'm fine," Rowan said. "Just in shock."

"What happened?" the man asked.

"I don't know."

When the man got back into his car, Rowan opened her door and stepped out. Her knees buckled under her, and she grabbed on to the roof for support.

She looked up at the sky, took a few steps away from the car, and yelled at the top of her lungs. Then she collapsed on the ground, weeping. "God help me," she said over and over until she fell asleep.

When Rowan woke in the middle of the night, it was dark along the side of the highway. No cars passed, and the stars were covered by a swell of clouds. She lifted her head and looked around confused.

It took a minute for her eyes to adjust to the darkness. But before she was able to locate the car, she heard a rhythmic beeping from inside; she had left the driver's door ajar.

Rowan staggered over to the car and sat inside. Her cellphone was flashing.

She drove back toward the city, staring ahead soberly.

When she got to the hotel, she listened outside Tony and Sasha's door but heard nothing so went inside her own room. In the mirror, Rowan could see a red light flashing on the desk phone, indicating that there was a message. She touched the mirror, then the bed, then her suitcase, as if she had just been blindfolded and was checking that all the things in the room were where she had left them.

Rowan listened to the phone messages. It was Tony calling

about the drinks, then calling to see where she was, then calling because he was worried.

Rowan knocked on Tony and Sasha's door. She heard some rustling, then Tony stepped out.

"Where the hell were you?" Tony slurred. He was drunk. His eyes bloodshot, his clothes stinking of tobacco and pot. Before she could answer, Tony stumbled to Rowan's door and they went inside. He opened the mini-bar and grabbed a beer and a little bottle of Scotch. He offered the beer to Rowan.

"I don't want anything to drink."

"Suit yourself," Tony said.

"I have to tell you something," Rowan said.

Tony opened the beer can and took a sip.

"I have to tell you something very important. You're probably not going to believe me, but I have to tell someone."

"Shoot," Tony slurred.

"I rented a car and drove for a while along the highway toward the mountains."

"You still got the car?" Tony asked.

"Yes," Rowan said.

Tony's eyes were heavy.

"Something happened to me," Rowan said, slightly irritated. But the beer fell from Tony's hand, and she didn't attempt to retrieve it because he had passed out.

* * *

In the morning, Rowan woke up to the sound of Tony vomiting in the bathroom. Rowan had slept face down on her bed with her clothes on.

Although he had the faucet running, Rowan could still make out the noise of Tony dry heaving. She was looking out the window when he emerged from the bathroom.

"Oh God, let me die now," Tony said, and collapsed on the unmade bed where he had slept. "Where were you last night?"

"Nowhere."

"You were gone a long time. I don't even remember coming in here last night."

"Do you think you should tell Sasha where you are?" Rowan asked. "She'll worry."

"Let her sleep," he said. "She was up half the night worried about you."

"I'm sorry," Rowan said.

"What's wrong with you?" Tony asked, and curled into a ball and put a pillow over his face.

"Nothing. I'm tired. I didn't get a good night's sleep either. What do you want to do today?" Rowan asked.

"Doesn't matter," Tony said. "Let Sasha decide."

Rowan walked into the bathroom. The room smelled of bile, and there were dribbles of vomit around the toilet. The fan buzzed above her head, and the throbbing from yesterday came back. She dug into her toiletries bag for some painkillers and took them both in a single swig.

Sasha was wearing a bathrobe and had her hair wrapped in a towel when she opened the door. "Where's Tony?"

"Sleeping in my room. He's sick, so I let him sleep."

"Did he tell you he won five hundred dollars?" Sasha asked.

"No," she said.

"We were worried about you," Sasha said.

"I don't know what to do." Rowan started to weep, and Sasha held her in her arms.

"I know," she said. "It's been hard for you. Divorce is never easy."

"No, no. It's not that."

"What is it?" Sasha asked.

"If I say, you'll think I'm crazy."

"Try me."

"I can't. I can't say. I'm alone."

"You're not alone."

"Yes, I am. I'm totally alone in this, and I don't know what to do."

Sasha put her hands on Rowan's cheeks to calm her.

Wiping her eyes, Rowan stepped away from Sasha. "I'm sorry. I shouldn't have done that. I shouldn't be crying like a baby."

"Honey, you can come to me about anything. I've known you longer than your own baby sister."

"I will tell you," Rowan said. "But not now. I know I can trust you, but the time is not right. I've got to let this settle. To think it through. If I act impulsively, it could cause trouble."

Sasha hugged Rowan. There were tears in her eyes.

Tony came into the room. "I feel like shit," he said. He opened the mini-fridge and grabbed a beer.

Sasha looked at him in disgust. "That's what alcoholics do," she said.

"Not everyone is an alcoholic," Tony said.

They decided to drive to a restaurant the hotel brochure recommended for breakfast.

Unbelievably, the sedan did not have a scratch on it from the previous night's accident, which made Rowan wonder if what she had experienced had been real. She was so distracted she could hardly converse.

Tony had to get Sasha to pull over so he could vomit at the side of the road.

"You need to unload whatever burden you're carrying," Sasha said to Rowan while she kept her eye on Tony, who was holding on to the side of the car.

"I can't," Rowan said.

"What happened to you?" Sasha asked.

"I don't know."

Tony was too sick to eat in a restaurant, so Rowan dropped them off at the hotel and told Sasha she was going for another drive.

She found the spot where her car had skidded by the tire marks she'd left in the middle of the highway.

Rowan approached the area as hesitantly as she would approach the gravesite of a loved one and started taking pictures with the digital camera that Manny had bought her several years ago. Then she sat in the car, looking at the horizon, trying to will the vision to return.

She was interrupted by Sasha calling wanting to make dinner plans, but Rowan said she couldn't make it.

"Maybe we can all have a drink later?" Sasha asked.

"Maybe," Rowan said, and hung up.

Rowan drove to Fremont Street and went into a casino. Regulars and tourists were at the slots near the front.

Rowan sat at a table by the back and ordered a Scotch. Her breathing was laboured, so she took her inhaler. Alcohol wasn't good for asthma, but she drank anyway.

After two double shots, Rowan slumped her head forward and sat like that, with her eyes shut, for a long time. Briefly she worried about the car and how she would get back to the hotel, but she let the thought drift upward like a helium balloon.

At the bar a small TV was playing a sitcom she didn't recognize. When the studio audience laughed, Rowan laughed too, even though she had no idea what was funny.

"Something terrible happened to me," Rowan said out loud.

"Something terrible has happened to us all," a booming voice said behind her. Rowan turned and saw a woman about who looked about eighty taking the last sip from her beer glass. She was spry and frail at the same time.

"If I tell you, you'll think I'm crazy."

"Then don't tell me," the woman said, and pulled up a chair. "And if you do, I won't remember anyway."

"I've seen the end of the world."

"Everyone sees the end of the world. It's how we accept death," the woman said.

"But I know what's going to happen to everyone and everything," Rowan said.

The woman looked at Rowan with a flicker of recognition. "That's fantastic," she laughed. "That's really terrific. You hear that, Sue?" she said to the bartender.

Sue groaned and brought a tray of drinks to the slot machine players.

Rowan's eyes became large with tears.

"Ohhh, dear. It sounds to me like you want to be special before it's all too late," the woman said, touching Rowan's hand tenderly.

Rowan didn't think the woman had intended to be cruel, but it hurt and embarrassed her all the same. It was the same feeling of shame she had experienced as a child when her father would tell her she was attention-seeking or making something "all about" her. Was she making the end of the world all about herself?

The woman dropped her smile. "I believe you," she said seriously. "I can tell you're not messing around."

"Should I tell somebody?" Rowan asked.

The woman thought about it for a long while. "No. Don't. You better not."

"Why?

"Although they say they do, nobody wants to know what's going to happen next. They don't want to know they'll lose at the casino any more than they want to know what alcohol does to the body. I know and still I drink," she laughed, lifting up her empty glass.

"Do you want to know?" Rowan asked.

The woman shook her head. "You know what I'm going to do? I'm going to have a good time until the bitter end."

"It's a big secret to keep," Rowan said.

"Yes," the woman said, "and it's all yours."

TWO FRIENDS ON A BEACH

Two friends on a beach on a hot day.

A: It was supposed to be breezy this afternoon.

B: And now it's hot.

A: Wait up for me. You're going too fast.

B: Hurry up. You're slowing me down.

A: It hurts.

B: What hurts?

A: Everything hurts, but it's my foot at the moment.

B: You better come swimming.

A: I told you I'm not swimming.

B: Yes you are.

A: Did you bring the blanket? I'm going to read on the blanket.

B: If you come swimming, I'll give you the blanket.

A: Bribery.

B: Negotiation.

A: Why do you care if I come in or not?

B: I don't want to go alone. I don't want to be alone.

A: We're *all* alone.

B: Don't be morbid.

A: "We're born alone, we live alone, we die alone. Only through our love and friendship can we create the illusion for the moment that we're not alone." Orson Welles said that.

B: Has he ever heard of childbirth and mothers? It's not like babies just pop out of the ground. It's impossible to be born alone. And basically no one lives alone. Welles needed people to take care of him because he couldn't take care of himself. I understand the quote as a feeling of loneliness, but it doesn't stand up to an ounce of scrutiny.

A: Yes, but aren't you terrified of what the universe has in store for you?

B: I just live my life. I go to work. I go to the gym. I make dinner for myself. Sometimes I visit my aging parents.

A: I drink too much, I worry about drinking too much, and then I think about death. Is that normal?

B: No one's normal. You know, I just wanted you to come swimming with me, and you turned it into a philosophical debate.

A: I'm in a constant state of dissatisfaction. I'm midway through my life and I find myself in a dark forest and the straightforward path is lost to me.

B: Dante?

A: He may have said it first, but I'm standing here looking at the trees, and, well, they don't look so good. They look kind of sick actually.

B: Maybe they need water.

A: Maybe they need to be something other than trees.

B: It's October, and I can't believe I'll be swimming in the lake.

A: Did you like *Citizen Kane*?

B: It's a classic.

A: I kind of found it boring. Actually, I fell asleep during it, and if someone put a gun to my head, I couldn't tell them the plot.

B: It's a classic.

A: What exactly did you like about it?

B: I don't know.

A: You just like it because it's been named the best film of all time.

B: You're being confrontational. I thought you and your shrink were working on that.

A: I've decided I like who I am now. Even my flaws—even my bad personality.

B: There's no helping you.

A: The water is too cold. I bet you'll freeze.

B: Come on. Get in the water with me. The water's warm.

A: It's warm in October because of pollution and climate change.

B: Don't ruin a good day with bad news.

A: In the grand scheme of life, it doesn't matter if I go in or not. Being here is just another moment that passes. You go in the water. I don't go in the water. It makes no difference because we both are going to die. So is the pigeon over there, for that matter. Is it possible to hate a bird this much? I guess I hate Canada geese more.

B: I feel like we had this same conversation when we were fifteen. Do you remember that summer night when we snuck into our old elementary school playground and smoked menthol cigarettes and talked about our future? We wondered if we would be happy or if our lives would turn out the way we wanted them to. Do you remember that conversation?

A: I'm not keeping track of our conversations. Sometimes we argue the same points. Sometimes we have the opposite opinion.

B: We wondered if people got what they deserved or if we are just living in random chaos. Canada geese shit green. I've stepped in it before.

A: Did you know that birds are dropping from the sky?

B: Birds?

A: Birds are dropping from the sky and we're worried about the price of gas or what the housing market is like.

B: What kind of birds?

A: Snow geese. On their trek from Russia, they're dropping out of the sky from pure exhaustion. People have found them—skinny and tired and injured—and have brought them to a sanctuary.

B: I'm not afraid of dying. It's the suffering I worry about. My cat is so old he can't even jump on the dining room table anymore.

A: Fundamentally there is something wrong with life. The whole concept. It was just a bad idea. I give life a D minus.

B: Do you think you will have any regrets?

A: Of course. Who doesn't have regrets? But the wonderful thing about life is that no matter what you feel about your life or someone else's life, it doesn't make any difference. Happy or sad. Content or discontent. Having saved the world or polluted it. Even the asshole in the BMW who cuts you off in traffic and almost hits a cyclist—even how he feels about his life doesn't matter in the end. We put so much importance on feelings while we're living, and feelings in the end matter less than anything else.

B: What can we do then?

A: Not much.

B: We can pay attention to the natural world. It needs us. It's in trouble.

A: If it makes you feel better to recycle or watch birds or go for a swim, then good for you.

B: I'm going in the water.

A: Okay.

B: I'm leaving you behind.

A: I'm ready for it.

B: You'll be alone and I'll be alone.

A: Yes, that's right, and don't forget I wanted to be alone.

B: The illusion will be broken.

A: That's okay. I was never illuded.

BIRDS

I'm trying to distract myself by thinking of birds flinging themselves against glass windows. It's a sad state of affairs.

Some survive, but many don't.

There are things that can be done to prevent this so the birds don't see the sky reflected in the glass, but most people don't bother to do anything about it.

Why should they care about something that will never affect them?

People are not birds. They don't fling themselves against glass. Right?

THE DAY THE WORLD ENDED

The day the world ended was the same day my laptop and cellphone were stolen. I was at the library working on an important project when two teenagers approached me. They knew my name and said my husband was their teacher. I stood up to talk to them. They said they recognized me and we had met before at an art opening. I didn't recognize them, but I played along.

It's embarrassing when someone knows you but you don't know them. Meanwhile, three middle-aged strangers stood over my workspace, passing my laptop back and forth between them.

"I'm not done here," I said to them.

One of them set my laptop down and then they all walked away without a word. When I went to pack up my laptop, I noticed it wasn't my laptop on the table. I felt in my coat for my phone and the phone I pulled out wasn't mine.

I screamed. "Someone has taken my laptop and my phone! I've been robbed!"

Everyone in the library turned to stare, but no one said or did anything to help me. I tried to see which way the three strangers had gone; they were nowhere in sight. Even the two teenagers I'd been talking to had disappeared.

I remembered that I had saved my banking passwords on my computer and felt deep regret. Those people were probably stealing my money as I stood in the middle of the library.

I ran down the stairs and approached the security office, but a sign said *Back in Five Minutes*.

A man was standing beside the security office. I held up the fake laptop.

"Someone stole my laptop," I said.

"Today the world is ending, so I wouldn't worry about it." He reached into his pocket and pulled out a cigarette and lighter and started to smoke.

"It's no smoking in the library," I said.

He turned his back to me and leaned against the wall.

"When the security comes, they'll tell you to put it out," I said.

"Security isn't coming back," he said.

"The sign says they will be back in five minutes."

"That was before the world started ending."

"Someone is stealing my money as we speak," I said.

"You won't need it anymore. No one needs money when the world ends."

"What do they need?" I asked.

"They need to hold on tight."

We're Not Here to Talk about Aliens

FLOWERS

When I was five and my parents were in the process of getting separated, I befriended our next-door neighbour, Joy, a single woman in her thirties. One day I helped her plant some new flowers that she bought for her garden. She taught me how to dig holes with a trowel and fill the holes with water before placing the plants in them. She explained how far apart the plants should be and how to carefully take them out of the plastic tray.

When we finished, she invited me into her house for a treat. Joy put on a folk music record and burned incense while we ate cookies and drank herbal tea with honey. She had a British accent and told stories about growing up in England and her sister who had contracted polio as a child. Her house was bright, and she had original artwork on the walls and healthy green spider plants hanging from her ceiling and palm trees and ferns the height of me in large, hand-painted pots on the floor. She clipped off a leaf and stem from her spiderwort plant and instructed me to place it in a glass of water and set it on a windowsill at home. When the roots grew, she would help me plant it.

The next day I walked by Joy's house, and she was very upset. Some animal had dug out all the flowers we had planted together. I eagerly helped her replant them and then we went inside her house for more tea, cookies, and music. She asked if I had put the clipping in water, and I told her I did and that I was taking good care of it, and I was. I tended to the clipping several times throughout the day, waiting for the roots to grow.

For the next couple of days, I walked by Joy's house, but she wasn't outside. I didn't dare knock on her door because I had no reason to. My mother had instructed me not to bother our neighbours.

Finally, when I couldn't stand it anymore, I went over to her garden and started pulling out all the flowers we had planted together. Then I ran up to her front porch, rang her doorbell, and told her the plants had been dug out again. I suggested that maybe it was squirrels or the boy who lives at the other end of the street who I had seen put eggs in people's mailboxes.

Joy was furious, but I helped her replant the flowers, and once again I was rewarded by being invited inside for a snack and to listen to music. I told her my clipping was starting to grow roots, and I wondered when we could plant it. "It's going to need more time," she said. "You have to be patient."

The following day, I did it again, but this time I waited for her to discover her torn-up garden before I offered my help. She said, "If this keeps up, the flowers will die, and I'm going to have to cover everything in bushes and cedar chips." Her voice cracked, like she was trying to hold back tears.

This threat of her covering up her garden gave me pause. In fact, I avoided walking by her house altogether, so that I wouldn't be tempted to rip out the flowers and harm them. I thought about Joy's flowers and garden night and day.

After almost a week of not going near her house, I found myself standing over her garden. I wanted to stop myself, but I couldn't. I felt like I was being propelled forward by some kind of force field or a magnetic pull. I wanted to spend time with Joy, and the only way I believed she would spend time with me was if I was of use to her. It didn't occur to me she probably would have spent time with me had I simply asked.

I thought about how she planned to put in bushes and cedar chips if her garden kept being destroyed. I thought about how horrible it would be if there were no more bright, colourful flowers. Everyone agreed she had the most beautiful garden on the street. She chose flowers that would be beneficial to pollinators, and because of this her garden was abundant with bees, butterflies, moths, and other insects, all of which she identified using their scientific names.

Kneeling down in front of Joy's flowerbed, I began ripping out the flowers I loved so much by their roots. I tried to be careful, but it was impossible not to damage the most fragile among them.

"It was you all along," I heard Joy say above me in a sharp tone. She was standing on her porch, hands on her hips, looking down at me in disbelief.

I had been caught.

Although it had crossed my mind to tell her I was replanting them, I had no idea how long she had been watching me, and by the look on her face, she had seen it all.

I dropped the fistful of flowers I held and ran back home to hide underneath a bush in our front garden, an overgrown flowerbed no one tended to.

Joy marched over to my house and told my mother what I had done.

"She's been pulling out my flowers for weeks and pretending to help me replant them. She's a very devious little girl," Joy said.

My mother was mortified and explained that she and my father were separating and it had been very hard on me. She offered to pay for new flowers, but Joy refused.

Although I didn't get punished, my mother did make me knock on Joy's door the next day and apologize. "You need to own up to your mistakes," my mother said. "It's the right thing to do."

I brought over the clipping Joy had given me. A couple of small roots were beginning to grow, and I wanted to show her how they were coming along.

When she opened the door and saw me, she did not greet me with her usual big smile. Instead she had a stern frown. She did not like me anymore, and I knew it.

I told Joy I had come to apologize for pulling out her flowers. "I don't know why I did it," I said, "but I'm very sorry."

She thanked me quickly, then shut the door before I had a chance to say goodbye.

I stood on her porch for a few moments, stinging with regret. It was a painful sting that felt worse than if I had been stung by a bee.

Looking at the clipping in my hand, I knew we'd never plant it together, so I set it down on the small ledge of her front door, hoping she would plant it when the roots fully formed and were strong enough to take hold.

TRADING CARDS

The summer before I went to kindergarten, my dad packed up a large suitcase and left. He lived with us and then he lived somewhere else—a tiny bachelor apartment with a small black-and-white TV on the other side of town.

My parents acted like the separation was perfectly normal, nothing to get upset about. My dad would take me out for dinner for an hour once a week. Seeing him infrequently was not all that bothersome because it meant fewer fights between my parents. When they fought it was awful, scary. He would throw things, and she would drink until she passed out

The day after a blowout, my mother would ask if I was okay, and my father would stammer his idea of an apology—a list of excuses that always ended with "Your mother made me do it."

My mother and I lived in a small one-floor house in a wealthy part of town. The closest school was predominantly populated by rich or upper-middle-class white kids whose parents were married. Anyone who was not like them was either bullied or ignored.

I had an eyelid that drooped, a birth defect. At the beginning of the school year, many of the kids asked why my eye was droopy. Could I see out of it? Would it ever get better?

I answered these questions until their curiosity was satisfied. Soon, though, their curiosity turned to taunting and teasing, pulling up and down their own eyelids to mimic my "lazy" eye. I quickly discovered that if I said nothing, eventually they would move on to someone else, like a cat who tires of a dead bird.

At the back of the kindergarten was a miniature fast food

station, a miniature kitchen, and a miniature doctor's office where the students would engage in imaginative role-playing games. The front of the room was for story time, singing, and show and tell, and the round tables in the middle of the room for arts and crafts.

While my classmates interacted with me inside the classroom, at recess I was on my own. The popular game at the time was a form of tag where either girls chased boys or boys chased girls. I often sat with my back against the grey building and watched them run around the schoolyard laughing, picking on each other and sometimes breaking out into fist fights.

Each Friday was show and tell—the only time I actually had to get up in front of the class and speak. For the first show and tell, I brought in my favourite stuffed animal, a monkey with a plastic face and hands that held a plastic banana. The class was mildly interested. Some kids asked me a few polite questions, like where did I get it or what was its name.

The next week, I brought the monkey in again and talked about him as if I hadn't just brought him in the week before. Everyone, including the teacher, was confused, but they played along and asked me the exact same questions.

I did this every week until James brought in his pet hamster and upped the show-and-tell game tenfold. The hamster put the class into a near frenzy. Books and rocks and small toys were no longer going to do it. The next week, Jess brought in her father, a firefighter, who let everyone try on his leather helmet, and Kara brought in ballet slippers and performed beautifully for the class. I absolutely could not bring my monkey in again. I had come to realize that show and tell had stakes attached. Whether kids liked you or were interested in you had more to do with what you had to offer in this weekly exercise in humiliation than anything else.

I asked my mother if I could bring in our cat, Smokey, a

rough outdoor cat. She immediately said no because it wouldn't be fair to him. "Think of his feelings," she said, "and how scared he would be around so many children. Also he might bite someone."

I looked around my room for something that would be awe-inspiring and make the kids like me. Another stuffed animal was not an option. Nor was a book.

What did I have that was worth talking about?

I scanned my room.

And then I spotted one of my most prized possessions: my collection of *Charlie's Angels* trading cards.

The hefty stack of cards was as thick as two encyclopedias. I held them together with a broad blue elastic. Each day I shuffled the cards around and organized them into various groups—by character or by theme or by duplicates. I tried to keep them neat and undamaged, but a few were well-worn.

Once I decided to bring my *Charlie's Angels* cards for show and tell, I looked forward to going to school for the first time. I had butterflies in my stomach and could hardly sleep. I was more excited about this than I was about Christmas. I imagined doing my presentation—my classmates looking at me in astonishment as they asked me all sorts of questions for which I had prepared the answers. How long had I been collecting? How did I get so many? How did I organize them? Which one was my favourite?

I had to really think about which one was my favourite. Farrah Fawcett was an obvious choice, but I actually liked Kate Jackson the best because she seemed funny and smart and because I liked her name. My big decision was whether I would pretend to like Farrah the best or announce that Kate was the angel I preferred.

Though I didn't get much sleep, I bounced out of bed in the morning and got ready for school without my mother having to ask me to do a thing. I washed my face and brushed my teeth and combed my hair and picked out my best outfit—a polyester T-shirt with a photograph of a lion on it and corduroy pants. For the first time in my life, I was looking forward to something that I knew would be great.

At school I was quiet, not because I felt shy but because my mind was racing in anticipation of my future stardom on the show-and-tell platform. Going through the motions of the national anthem, the Lord's Prayer, story time, and arts and crafts, which I usually enjoyed, was excruciating. Finally, after the snack break, we all gathered around on the blue carpet at the front of the room.

When Miss Alma asked for volunteers, my hand shot up for the first time all year, but she called on Brad instead. Brad stood up with a big grin on his face.

"This is going to be awesome," he said as he walked to the cloakroom and brought out a plastic portable record player and three singles—one by ABBA, one by Diana Ross, and one by Queen. The class gasped because Brad had not only outdone himself and everyone else—he had exquisite taste in music. His brother was a DJ, he admitted.

While the other children laughed and danced and sang with a fervour none had ever experienced in their short lives, I stood still, burning with resentment at being upstaged by that portable record player.

Once Brad's turn was over, Miss Alma called on me.

I was filled with dread as I walked over to my cubby to retrieve the *Charlie's Angels* cards and slowly made my way to the front of the room.

The class was still excited from Brad's presentation. They were laughing and chatting and comparing their favourite music with one another. Miss Alma had to ask them several times to quiet down so I could begin my presentation.

In almost a whisper, I said, "*Charlie's Angels* is my favourite

TV show, and I collected these trading cards." I held up the stack. I didn't even remove the elastic or show a single card. "Every time I go to the store with my mother," I said, "she buys me a pack. My parents are legally separated," I told the class nonchalantly. "So my dad buys me some too."

"What's 'separated'?" a kid asked.

"It means they don't live together anymore," I said. I was beginning to realize the separation was not as ordinary as my parents had made it out to be.

"Why?" someone else asked.

"Because they don't love each other and they fight." As I said this out loud, I suddenly felt sad about it for the first time. The pain of my family situation was hitting me now in the middle of what was supposed to be the presentation of my life.

I looked over at the teacher helplessly.

Finally, Miss Alma intervened. "Does anyone have any questions about the trading cards?"

The class stared at us both blankly. I could hear the whistle of the gym teacher in the schoolyard. I could smell someone's feet, and I felt both a little dizzy and a little sick.

Then one kid said, "Do you ever see your dad anymore?"

"Sometimes. He takes me out for dinner once a week. If my mom is drinking too much, I stay over at his apartment until she feels better," I blurted, then immediately regretted.

"You have a wonderful collection," Miss Alma said quickly. "Thank you for sharing it with us."

I sat back down and held the cards in my hand. They felt like lead. My face was hot, my hands throbbing. I couldn't get rid of the lump in my throat that had formed.

At recess, I sat in my usual spot at the side of the school near the door. I held back my tears with all the strength I could muster. Eventually the desire to cry subsided, and I shuffled through my cards unenthusiastically.

I had bombed, and I knew it.

Although I could stop myself from sobbing, I couldn't control the tears falling down my cheeks silently, but no one noticed.

Tiff was the one student who everyone wanted to be friends with. Her parents were hippies. She wore the nicest clothes and everyone wanted to play with her at recess.

She walked over to me and asked if she could look at my cards. She liked the TV show too.

I handed her the deck and watched as she examined each card.

"You have doubles," she said.

"Yeah," I said.

"Can I have one?" she asked.

I brightened at her interest. "Sure."

She took the card—the one framed in red where the Angels are holding guns. Then she went to play with the others again.

She showed Alyssa the card I had given her, and they pointed at me. Kim came over and asked for one too, so I gave it to her. "Are you sure?" she asked. And I nodded as she skipped away to join the others.

Another kid came and then another and another, and soon the whole class was surrounding me, asking for a card, then demanding a better card, then asking for more than one, then the kids began to fight over their cards.

Interestingly no one took a card unless I told them they could. But they were relentless in their asking, so I felt like I couldn't say no. There was an exchange going on here, their favour for my cards.

As soon as they got what they wanted, all the kids took off again and returned to their play.

My brief brush with popularity was not what I had imagined. Miss Alma had been on the other side of the schoolyard talking to another teacher. She walked over to me. "What's going on over here?"

I knew enough not to be a snitch, so I said nothing.

She looked down at the empty blue elastic in my hands and asked where my cards had gone.

"I gave them to all my friends," I said.

She called out to the students and waved them over. They all loved her, so they did as they were told. "You must give the cards back," she said gently. She never had to yell like I'd seen other teachers do.

The kids—if they could have expressed their feelings like adults—would have said they were pissed.

Some tossed the cards at me indifferently, others more kindly placed them in my hands. One kid said sorry, another threw a card at my face. As quickly as they had been distributed, the cards were back in my hand, fastened together snuggly with the blue elastic.

Miss Alma offered to keep the cards safe until the end of the day, and I was relieved to be rid of them for a while. "But don't bring them to school again," she said softly.

She meant it kindly, I'm sure—so that no one would take them from me, but that's not how I interpreted her words, which felt a criticism, like I had done something unimaginable and terribly wrong.

BIKE AND THE FIRE HYDRANT

I was nine years old and riding my two-wheel bike on the sidewalk of our small street. I don't know how it happened—perhaps I wasn't paying attention or I had gotten overconfident in my bike-riding ability—but I slammed into a yellow fire hydrant at full speed and smashed my pubic bone on the bar of my bike.

Until then I didn't know you could feel pain greater than a skinned knee or a sore throat. This was even worse than the pain of all the eye operations. I felt it head to toe. It had no beginning and no ending.

No one saw me, so I had no need to cry.

Instead, I held my crotch the way I had seen boys do when they were kicked in the balls.

WE'RE NOT HERE TO TALK ABOUT ALIENS

There was a planetarium beside the old public library and once a year our elementary school teachers would take us there.

We'd remove our coats and boots and lie on the floor on our backs in a circle, and they would show us the planets and constellations and talk about the solar system.

One kid asked about aliens, to which our teacher replied, "We're not here to talk about aliens."

The planetarium smelled like bad breath and dust.

You could hear everyone breathing and sniffling because it was winter. The girl beside me wiped her runny nose on the sleeve of her shirt.

I shut my eyes until I fell asleep because I preferred to not think about such things as myself in relation to the universe.

THE PAD

When I was ten, I stuck one of my mother's unused maxi-pads to my bedroom wall.

It had fallen out of the linen closet and was just lying on the bathroom floor. When I saw it there, I peeled off the paper strip and stuck the pad to the wall.

I didn't care who saw my wall art—my mom, my best friend, my sister.

I didn't feel shame because I didn't know there was anything to be ashamed about. I knew about periods and that pads were there to soak up the blood.

"It's a pad. Who cares?" I said when anyone inquired. "It's a beautiful piece of art," I laughed.

My pad art delighted me until one day my mom's friend from university and her daughter were visiting from out of town.

The daughter, Emma, was a year older than me. Her long red hair and freckled face could be found every year on the Christmas card that her mother sent. Not a picture of the family—just Emma, who she bragged endlessly about in the letter. Emma was perfect in every sense of the word. She got straight As, was on the girls' basketball team, was popular, artistic, and beautiful.

Emma was also the kind of person who spoke in a way that made you think she was always making fun of you. Little private inside jokes to herself.

She would say things like, "Where did you get those shoes?" in a must-have tone about a pair of old dirty runners.

"The BiWay."

"Right." She nodded like she was storing the information for a future dig.

Around Emma, I was a clumsy ugly duckling who was just trying to get through these visits without making a fool of myself or getting ridiculed.

The only thing that made Emma and me remotely friends or connected in any way was that both of our mothers were alcoholics. When they drank together it was even worse than when each drank alone. They would get sloppy, crying, fighting drunk and pass out, leaving cigarettes burning in the ashtray, lights on, the record player spinning.

Emma's visits were about the only time I cleaned my messy bedroom. I displayed cool things around my room that I thought would impress Emma, like my sticker books, my teen magazines, my B-52's records.

But when Emma came into my room, the first thing she saw was the pad. "Why do you have a maxi-pad on your wall?" she asked.

She was not impressed. She did not think it was funny or that it was art.

Mortified, I ripped the pad down and said, "I didn't want to lose it."

Shame washed over me as I squeezed the pad in my hand, wishing I could be someone else, wishing I hadn't done such a strange thing.

"Aren't you young to have a period?" she asked.

"I don't have a period. I just have a pad on my wall."

We moved on to other topics, but I could tell that something had shifted.

Not only was I an ugly duckling, but I was also now weird and gross. And once someone decides you are weird and gross, like the kids who pick their noses or shit their pants at school, there's no going back.

"Are they drinking?" I asked, hoping to rekindle our connection about our moms.

"My mom doesn't drink anymore," Emma said.

Emma wouldn't look at me for the rest of the visit. I was strange and she was not. She was normal and I was not. She sat in the living room, listening to our moms reminisce while I stayed in my room too embarrassed to join them.

After Emma and her mother left, I looked down at the pad, which remained crumpled on my bed.

I smoothed it out and was about to put it back on the wall but thought maybe I should put it somewhere less obvious, like behind my bedroom door or under the desk or beside my window.

None of these places pleased me. It just wasn't the same.

At one point I even threw it out because the adhesive began to lose its stickiness, and it kept falling off the wall.

But my bedroom looked empty without the maxi-pad, so I pulled it out of the trash and used masking tape to secure it back in its original place.

STICKERS

My best friend Thea and I were allowed to walk downtown to the sticker store and shop for stickers when she was twelve and I was eleven.

We bought scratch-and-sniff stickers and puffy stickers with googly eyes and stickers of pineapples and stickers of flowers and stickers that said *Wow* and stickers with smiley faces. Some stickers cost ten cents and better ones cost twenty. The most expensive sticker in the sticker store was seventy-five cents.

Choosing stickers was a long and painful process. We didn't want the same stickers, but also we didn't want our stickers to be too different from each other, lest we become jealous and regret our own purchases.

Some stickers were for our pencil cases. Other stickers were for the front of our spelling notebooks. The rest landed in our sticker albums, where we would not look at them until our next trip to the sticker store.

One day after an hour spent shopping and another twenty minutes spent at the candy store, we walked toward home, pleased with ourselves and our purchases, chatting about dinner—would she come to my house or would I go to hers?

As we walked along the busy sidewalk, a man in his twenties, wearing loose grey jogging pants, flashed us when he walked by.

Shocked and revolted, we looked at each other, then burst out laughing.

BARBIE DOLLS

No one could figure out exactly who had molested me that first time. For one thing, I didn't tell anyone until five years after it happened.

Cynthia was a teenager who lived on our small street. She was six years older than me and acted like an older sister to me. Sometimes I would go over to her house and we would watch sitcoms together or listen to music. Sometimes she painted my fingernails.

She had long feathered hair, and I loved watching her get ready to go on dates. She always had boyfriends and she always complained about them.

On her date nights, Cynthia put on makeup and curled her hair and changed her clothes over and over. She had me rank her outfits and asked my advice on the jewellery she should wear. Sometimes she and her boyfriend went to a drive-in movie, other times they'd go to a party. Her life seemed glamorous.

One afternoon, she was getting rid of all her old Barbie dolls and had them in a pile in the middle of her rec room floor. I must have said something about the naked Ken doll because one minute we were sorting through her dolls, and the next she asked me, in the most serious tone I had ever heard her use, if anyone had ever touched me.

The problem with me is that I cannot lie, and she knew immediately that someone had touched me. In fact, it had happened again a few weeks earlier, but I couldn't bear to think about the most recent occurrence, so I told her about the first time, when I was five, assuming that because it had happened so long ago no one would care. But she did care and made me tell her everything.

When my parents got divorced, my mother hired Vye to sit with me over lunch hour and after school. Vye and her husband lived in a big house in the suburbs with their four kids. She often invited me over on weekends. I became so close with her and her family that she was a second mother to me and her kids were like siblings.

One weekend I was at Vye's house watching TV with her teenage son Greg and a friend of his who I had never seen before. The friend left and her son went to get ready for work. I was alone in the basement watching TV when the friend came back and knocked on the screen door, claiming he forgot something. I let him in, and when he found out Greg was in the shower, he molested me.

Despite my protests, Cynthia told my mom, who sat across from me in the living room. My mother interrogated me with questions like I was one of her clients. My mother was a social worker.

The questions were fired at me one after the other. I felt shame and disgust as I answered them.

No one could think of who the friend could be since none of their friends matched the description I gave, and I never saw the friend in their house again.

Given that there was no suspect, my mother decided not to pursue it further. "I'm not going to put you through that," she said, knowing full well what it would entail.

"Since it only happened once, you won't be scarred for life," my mother declared in her social worker voice, hoping that saying this would make it so.

FREIGHT

On our yearly visits to Peterborough to see my grandparents, I tried to avoid my grandmother as much as possible. She didn't think I was very bright. She didn't think my mother worked enough with me, and so, in the week we spent there, she was determined to make me smarter. She brought out flash cards and made me do spelling bees for money. "You can't add in your head," she would say. "How will you learn to play Yahtzee if you can't add in your head?"

I liked being with my grandfather best. He greased back his hair and smelled of whisky and tobacco.

On the drive to Peterborough, my mother sipped from a can of pop that was filled with vodka. I worried a lot on those trips. I worried that something bad would happen to my mother, and I'd be forced to drive the car. Or else I'd worry that I'd get appendicitis and my mother wouldn't get me to the hospital on time. Sometimes I was sure I felt the pains, but my mother always told me that I was fine, that if I had appendicitis, I wouldn't be able to walk.

There were things I was not supposed to tell my grandmother, like my marks or how fast my mother drove on the highway. I wasn't allowed to tell my grandmother about any of my mother's purchases, like the stereo she ordered and paid for on a rent-to-own basis, her trip to Las Vegas, and that she got her sweat glands removed.

My grandparents gave my mother money. They paid for her car and the dishwasher, and every year on her birthday they gave her a cheque. "When people give you money, they expect to control you," my mother told me.

* * *

"You're too thin, Vera. It's unhealthy to be that skinny," my grandmother commented to my mother the minute we walked through the door.

"How was the traffic?" my grandfather asked. He took a crumpled handkerchief from his pocket and blew his nose. His nose was red and looked sunburnt all the time.

My grandmother pulled me aside to ask how fast my mother had driven. I told her I didn't know, even though I had my eye on the speedometer the whole trip.

I watched my grandmother set the table with salad forks, cloth napkins, napkin rings, wineglasses, waterglasses, double plates, and miniature salt and pepper shakers in front of each place setting. At home we ate TV dinners on TV tables and watched game shows.

After dessert my mother excused herself to make phone calls. When she returned, she announced that she was going out with her old high school friend Margaret. I followed her to the spare room where we shared the pullout couch and asked if I could come with her.

"No, honey, you'd be bored," she said.

I watched her undress and put on deodorant. She still had scars under her arms from the sweat gland operation. She sprayed perfume on her neck and wrists and cleavage.

"Don't be late," my grandmother said. She stood in the hallway with a dishtowel over her shoulder.

My mother ignored her, then kissed me on the forehead before she headed out the door.

My grandmother went to bed while my grandfather and I watched *Lawrence Welk*. He rolled his cigarettes, set them one by one on the coffee table, then smoked in the bathroom during commercials.

At ten o'clock we turned in.

There were train tracks beside my grandparents' apartment building. I listened to the noises outside and waited for the sound of the train. Sometimes it took fifteen minutes to pass. Sometimes it stopped on the tracks and waited an hour before moving again—everything quiet and dark, the only sound my mother snoring on her side of the pullout couch. But not tonight.

At twelve o'clock, I still couldn't sleep. There was a park behind the apartment building that had monkey bars and a swing set. I put on my cords and sweatshirt and snuck downstairs.

The park was unlit, and I had to crawl through a hole in the fence to get to it. There wasn't anyone around, but I was nervous.

The swing was damp with dew, and my cords got wet when I sat down. I rubbed my initials in the dirt with the toe of my shoe and swung half-heartedly. I couldn't relax. I kept thinking that someone was watching me or that an animal was in a bush waiting to attack. I worried about rabies.

Standing on the swing, I looked at the tracks, hoping the train would come soon. I couldn't leave. As scared as I was, now that I was down here, I had to see the train. It took a long time to come, so long that I fell asleep on the swing with my head resting against the chain, and I awoke to the horn and the sound of the wheels against the tracks. The train was so close the whole ground was vibrating.

I watched the train until it became a speck in the distance and I couldn't hear it anymore. I crawled through the hole in the fence and ran all the way back to the apartment. When I got upstairs, I left my clothes on and climbed into bed, shivering.

My mother stumbled in at six o'clock and woke me up.

She smelled of beer.

* * *

My grandmother had breakfast ready on the table when I got up. Orange juice. Toast. Creamed cereal. Soft-boiled eggs. She asked what time my mother had got in, and I said I didn't know.

My mother finally emerged in the clothes she had worn the night before. Her eyes were smeared with mascara.

"Don't you look like something the cat dragged in," my grandmother said.

* * *

That night my mother took me to Margaret's birthday party at the lake. Margaret was hanging patio lanterns when we drove up.

My mother straightened her back as we approached the cottage and then pushed my shoulders back too.

The other guests hadn't arrived yet, so we helped set up, taking plastic cutlery, plates, and cups out of their wrappings and placing them neatly on the three picnic tables lined up in front of the cottage. My mother loaded warm beer into coolers filled with ice.

I wanted to go to the beach, but my mother wouldn't let me go by myself. "You're not a strong enough swimmer," she said.

Margaret made me a Shirley Temple and put three maraschino cherries in it. I heard somewhere that maraschino cherries gave you cancer but felt like I had to eat them because Margaret was staring at me. I didn't really understand about cancer but knew enough to know it was bad and not something I wanted. I thought I could feel the cancer invading my body as soon as I swallowed the first cherry. I couldn't believe my mother could just sit there and watch me eat something that could make me die.

I remembered seeing a religious show about a man who had cancer and was healed by God. He called it the big C and said he sat in a small room by himself every day and envisioned the cancer leaving his body. He said it was an act of God that he was cured.

When I told my mother about it, she said, "You can't believe everything you see on TV. Sometimes they pay people to say those things."

A few of the guests started to arrive, and Margaret's husband, Dermot, greeted them.

"She just treats me like a child. It's ridiculous," my mother said of my grandmother.

Margaret nodded sympathetically before standing to join her husband. "You'll persevere," she said in a condescending tone, which I don't think was what my mother wanted to hear. She grabbed herself another beer from the cooler and watched Dermot put his arm absent-mindedly around Margaret's shoulder.

"She drives me crazy too," I said.

My mother laughed. "It doesn't really affect you because she's not your mother. You're just lucky I tried so hard not to be like her."

I don't know when I noticed my mother getting drunk. Maybe it was when she started talking to that man, a friend of Dermot's. It seemed like one moment she was fine and the next she was slurring her words. It was the slurring that bothered me the most because then everyone else knew how drunk she was.

I went to the trailer beside the cottage where Margaret had set up a bed for me. But I couldn't sleep. I was bored and wanted to go back to my grandparents'.

Each time I bugged my mother, she said, "Just one more hour. I only get to see Margaret once a year."

But she wasn't talking to Margaret. She was talking to that

man with the dimple on his chin who I thought was ugly and was sitting way too close to my mother.

Around one o'clock everyone headed to the beach for a skinny-dip. The man asked my mother to go, and she said yes. She told me to hold her purse, and before she got away, I grabbed her arm. "I want to go home now."

"In a minute, honey." She staggered a bit and held on to Margaret for support.

"I'll tell Grandma you were drinking," I said, knowing this threat would make her leave.

As we walked to the car, my mother fumbled in her purse for her keys. When she turned to thank Margaret for a nice evening, she tripped and fell on her face.

Margaret, Dermot, and the man with the dimple rushed to her side. Margaret wiped at the grass stains on her knees. Someone picked up her purse and handed it to me.

"You okay to drive?" Margaret asked.

My mother laughed her off and got into the car.

I had driven with my mother when she was drunk many times, but this time was different. She wasn't in control of the car. We were on a dark gravel road in the country, and she was having trouble staying on one side. She kept drifting onto the shoulder, and I had to straighten the steering wheel.

She shook her head from side to side, trying to wake up. The car swerved again but this time into the lane of oncoming traffic. Luckily there weren't any cars on the road.

I was terrified we'd die.

I slapped my mother's face, pulled her hair, and pinched her arms to keep her from passing out.

It took us about an hour to get home. By the time we got into the city, my mother was driving so slowly that other cars were honking. It was better than speeding, though.

When we turned into my grandparents' parking lot, I was

relieved. I felt like someone who'd survived a near-death experience and was given a second chance at life—like how that man with cancer must have felt when he was finally cured. My mother was quiet in the elevator, and as soon as we got into the apartment she went to bed.

* * *

The next day, my grandparents took me department store shopping and bought me two shirts—one my grandmother picked out and one she let me pick out myself. My grandmother chose a frilly blouse with red and white pinstripes and a navy bow tie. I knew I'd have to wear it at least once during the visit. I picked a yellow T-shirt that said *DYNAMITE* in round neon letters.

My mother gave me the once-over when we got back to the apartment. "It's too big for her."

"I can take it back," my grandmother said.

"No, I like it," I said.

My mother felt the fabric with her thumb and forefinger.

My grandmother frowned. "You're not going out again tonight?"

My mother nodded. "I am."

I felt a bit sorry for my grandmother. She probably had hurt feelings. When my mother left the room to get ready, I didn't follow her. I was glad my mother was going out. I couldn't even look at her.

My grandmother must have sensed that something was wrong because she didn't bother me all night. No flash cards or spelling bees. We had a light supper of tuna sandwiches and watched TV.

That night the train came early. I was tired and fell asleep quickly. It was sometime around six in the morning when my grandmother came into the spare room and shook me awake. "Your mother's not back yet," she said.

A bobby pin fell out of her hairnet. She picked it up and bit the plastic tip between her teeth. She looked worried. No wonder no one tells her anything, I thought. She apologized for waking me up.

But she came in again at eight, announcing that my mother still wasn't home. My grandfather called Margaret, and when he found out that she wasn't there, my grandmother wanted to call the police. He told her to wait.

I spent the next few hours in the back room reading. I couldn't stand being with my grandparents. Every time the phone rang or there was a noise, my grandmother jumped up, expecting it to be my mother. My grandfather was calm. He smoked cigarettes on the balcony. My grandmother didn't make breakfast or lunch. Every hour that passed, she asked if they should call the police.

Around five, I came out of the spare room. My grandmother looked tired. I started to think about how it really wasn't like my mother not to call. Maybe she was dead or just wasn't coming back. Mothers abandon children all the time.

Then, without warning, I burst into tears. One moment I was at the fridge, hungry, and the next I was hysterical. My grandparents tried to calm me down. They told me all the places my mother could be and reasons why she couldn't get to a phone. They said how much she loved me and that she would never abandon me. My grandmother said that she was sure my mother wasn't dead, that she prayed to God, and He would never let it happen.

And then I told them everything. Once I started, I couldn't stop. I told them things I didn't even know I thought about, like how my mother passed out three or four times a week and left cigarettes burning in the ashtray, the men she brought home, the money she spent. I told them about the other night and how we were nearly killed and how she drove when she was drunk all the time, even on the highway. I told them I thought she might be dead.

My grandmother started to cry and then my grandfather had to soothe us both. It was close to seven. My grandfather said they should wait a little longer before he called the police.

For dinner we ate toast with butter and had glasses of warm milk. Even though it made my grandmother feel worse, I was glad I had told them everything. I thought things were going to change when my mother got back and that somehow my grandparents knowing would make my mother stop drinking.

Around nine o'clock my mother waltzed in. She went into the kitchen and got a pop out of the fridge. She acted like everything was normal. We stood there watching her, waiting for an excuse, anything.

But she just sat down on the couch.

I went back to the spare bedroom. Now that I knew she was okay, I felt silly for telling on her and a little guilty.

"She's a child. Children make things up. Don't listen to her." My mother's voice was loud.

This time my grandfather did all the talking. His voice was calm. He said he just wanted her to slow down, for my sake.

"I'm a social worker. I'm a damn good mother. How much do I drink? That's none of your business," my mother said over and over.

My grandmother suggested that my mother should take me to church.

"I don't take her to church because I don't believe in God."

This sent my grandmother running in tears to her bedroom.

My mother headed into the spare room where I was sitting on the couch and told me to pack my things.

"Why did you say those awful things?" she asked.

"I thought you were never coming back," I said.

* * *

My grandparents walked us to the car. I wondered if they thought us leaving was for the best.

My mother put the bags in the back, then got into the car and slammed the door. She turned the radio up so she couldn't hear anything.

I hugged my grandfather first. I would miss him. My grandmother squeezed me so tight I couldn't breathe, but I didn't mind. Then she flattened her handmade shirt with the palm of her hand. It was polyester and had an orange floral pattern on the front.

I could see that my grandmother was tired. I felt mean for worrying her.

I got into the back seat and waved. My grandparents waved back and tried to smile. I watched them the way I watched the train that night—only they were standing still, and I was moving farther and farther away. I watched them until I couldn't see their faces, until my grandmother's shirt became a small orange dot in the distance.

My mother hummed along to a song on the radio as she drove. As we passed the train tracks, I realized that tonight the train would come but I wouldn't be there to see it. I thought about the park and how scared I was at the time and how I would give anything to be there now, to feel the way the ground shook when I was so close to the train, to feel the cool chain of the swing pressed against my face, everything damp and wet and cold—completely alone, knowing that my grandparents were upstairs sleeping, so used to the sound of the train that they didn't even hear it.

BURNING SCHOOLHOUSE

One day as I was walking to school, I came upon a discarded burning-schoolhouse firework on the sidewalk, which was only burned on one side. A dud.

I glanced at it and then attempted to continue on my way until I was struck by a force within me that I could not control. The force pulled me back toward the firework and said, *You must touch this firework or everyone in your family will die.*

Each time I tried to walk away from the burning schoolhouse, I was convinced I was sealing the death of everyone I loved. Against my better judgment—because I knew fireworks could be dangerous—I touched it, and just like that the force that had controlled me completely went away.

Off I went to school, where I forgot about the burning schoolhouse until my walk home that afternoon, when I came upon it again. By this point the burning schoolhouse appeared to be flattened by a car or bike or someone's foot.

Once again, the force inside me said, *Touch the burning schoolhouse or everyone in your family will die.* However, this time when I touched the burning schoolhouse, the force did not go away. Instead, it grew bigger and bigger. First it told me to touch the burning schoolhouse ten times and then twenty and then thirty, until finally it said, *Bring the burning schoolhouse home or everyone in your family will die.*

As soon as I picked up the burning schoolhouse, the terrible force dissipated, and I immediately felt better again. I tried to put the burning schoolhouse in the garage, and then in the basement, but it demanded that it come inside the house and be placed in my clothes closet.

The next day it demanded to be placed inside my bed and then under my pillow and finally inside my pillowcase, where I had to sleep on it or everyone in my family would die.

The burning schoolhouse would not be satisfied. Each day it demanded more and more of me. It demanded that I touch it fifty, one hundred, two hundred times before I could do anything else.

It would not let me have a single moment of rest.

One day my mother found the burning schoolhouse in my pillowcase when she changed my sheets.

Upon discovering the burning schoolhouse was missing, I demanded to know where it was. She said she had thrown it in the trash and the garbage truck took it away.

I was inconsolable until my mother said, "If you don't calm down, I'm going to have to take you to the hospital."

Then she gave me cold milk with brown sugar in it and sent me to bed.

Before long, the burning schoolhouse became a distant memory, and I found other objects to touch—the toaster, the paring knife with the broken handle, bobby pins, the frozen metal fence outside my school—so I could keep everyone safe.

MY BODY

The first time I had sleep paralysis, I was eleven. It happened while I taking a nap in the middle of the day.

I floated atop my body, which wouldn't and couldn't move.

I could see myself sleeping and breathing as I hovered above. I could see the posters on the walls and the blue-and-red wallpaper. I could hear a dog barking outside and a child crying.

When I screamed to myself to wake up, I did not wake.

When I called for help, no one came.

I soon realized that if I wanted my body to do anything, I would have to return to it.

PUBLIC POOL

On a hot summer day when I was twelve and Thea was thirteen, we planned to go swimming at the public pool.

This was the first summer I was allowed to be alone while my mother was at work.

As usual I was running late, so Thea waited in the living room, watching cartoons while I put on my bathing suit.

When I took off my shorts, I found blood that had leaked through my underwear. Even though I knew immediately what it was because my mother had forced me to read *Are You There God? It's Me, Margaret*—I nonetheless screamed like I was in a horror movie.

Thea came running to the bathroom, thinking I had hurt myself.

"I got my fucking period," I cried.

Thea started laughing. She was older than me, but she had not yet gotten hers. "I thought you were dying," she said. "It's not a big deal."

"I don't want to be a woman!" I sobbed.

I called my mom at work. When the switchboard put her on the line and I heard my mom's voice, I wailed even louder than when I first discovered the blood.

"Calm down," she said gently. "I'll be right there."

I waited for her in the bathtub, thinking more blood was going to gush out of me at any minute, and Thea sat on the toilet seat to keep me company.

Thea asked what it felt like, and I choked out, "Terrible."

My mother came home and brought a box of pads. "You're too young for tampons," she said, and showed me how to place the pad in my underwear.

The pad, which smelled like cheap perfume, was made for an adult, not a twelve-year-old, and was uncomfortable to walk in.

"You'll get used to it," my mother said matter-of-factly.

My mother explained that my period would stop when I was in the water and that we could still go swimming.

"What if blood gets all over the place?" I asked, imagining the pool becoming a blood bath with swimmers screaming and pointing at me.

My mother told me to wear a pad, change at the pool, and then when I was done swimming, put in a new pad.

The plan was set. The day would be salvaged. I calmed down, somewhat, and my mother went back to work.

At the park, the pool was packed.

We hit the snack bar first, then laid out our blankets and ate Popsicles and SweeTarts and chips.

When we got hot enough, I snuck into the bathroom and removed my pad. Not too much blood had come out in the time it had taken us to ride down to the pool and eat our food.

But just in case, I kept my towel wrapped tightly around my waist.

"It looks like you're trying to hide something," Thea said.

"I am," I said.

Neither of us was a strong swimmer. We usually just stayed in the shallow end of the pool with all the little kids. We dipped in the pool, kicked around for a bit, competed in underwater breath-holding competitions, and then we got out to eat candy.

The swim was as uneventful as any other, but instead of lying in the hot sun to dry off, when we got out of the pool, I rushed into the bathroom to secure another pad. It felt gross to wear it with a wet bathing suit. I hadn't thought to bring a change of clothes.

Thea was lying on her back with her eyes shut when I returned from the change room.

"Let's go," I said, giving her a little nudge with my foot.

"No, I might want to go in again," she said.

"I just changed my pad," I said, annoyed. I sat down with the towel around my waist.

"Come in again."

"No, I don't have any more pads with me and I'm not going through all that again just for another swim."

Thea shrugged. "I'm hot."

I agreed to sit with my towel at the side of the pool and put my legs in the water.

Thea got in the pool. As I watched her hold her nose and put her head underwater, the tears came back. How free she looked, how much fun she was having.

When she got out, she wrapped her hair in a towel and we gathered up our belongings.

"Are you still upset?" she asked.

"No, I guess not," I said, and we headed home.

In the end, the day had turned out okay. It wasn't as bad as I thought it would be, but it wasn't all that great either.

A PERIOD STORY

Whenever I hear Christmas carols, I'm reminded of being twelve years old and having my period on the same night we had to go to Victoria Park with the Christian girls' group from the United Church to sing in front of the nativity scene, which was missing the baby Jesus because it had been stolen earlier in the week.

My friend Stacey was a member of the church and had been the one who invited me to join the group. It was an important night because we had been practising for weeks.

I am tone-deaf, and all the practising in the world couldn't help me, so I just mouthed along to the words to avoid making us sound bad, and no one seemed to notice.

I had my period earlier than other girls, and for some reason, I never took pain medication. I didn't think to tell my mom how bad the cramps were. I just suffered through it.

But that first year of my period, the pain was so severe I could hardly stand it. And this evening was no exception. It felt like someone was stabbing me repeatedly in the abdomen as I mouthed the words to "Jingle Bells" and "Silent Night" and "O Come All Ye Faithful."

At one point in the middle of "Jingle Bell Rock," I felt faint and saw stars in front of my eyes.

My hands were shaking and I began to sweat even though it was cold out.

I imagined being taken away in an ambulance and was most concerned—not that I would fall or smash my head—but that everyone would find out I had my period.

This was the same night I realized I hated God.

DESIRE

When Michael Manning was sixteen, and Thea and I were thirteen and twelve, we used to stand in front of his house and wait so we could catch a glimpse of him.

His father was a doctor, and they lived in a large brick house with an immaculate, manicured lawn. Not a blade of grass out of place, not a rose bush drooped or shrivelled.

Michael Manning would ride down our small street on his ten-speed, holding his tennis rackets in one hand and steering with the other, his dark hair tousled from the wind. When he passed us, we stopped everything we were doing and stared at him like he was a celebrity, and to us he was.

When he'd say hello or nod our way, we could hardly contain ourselves. Sometimes we got the nerve to say hello back, but mostly we waved and giggled.

He played tennis for the city and won championships. We knew whenever he had a tournament because he wore a bright white T-shirt, socks, and running shoes.

Thea and I played a game where one of us had to be Michael Manning and the other got to be his girlfriend, Madison, who we named after a character in our favourite Jackie Collins novel.

To be fair, we took turns playing Madison and Michael, acting out what Michael Manning and Madison would say to each other, what they would talk about on their dates. We dreamed up stories of how they got together and who liked who first. We created mini-dramas where Madison's ex-boyfriend tried to break them up or they had to leave town to attend different universities. Michael Manning would abandon his dream of being a tennis champion and study medicine like his father, and Madison would head to New York to be a journalist. Once Madison had a pregnancy scare but told Michael she was getting an abortion no matter what because they were rich and could afford to pay for one.

Michael Manning and Madison would almost break up several times, but then at the very last minute they would get back together, profess their love for each other, and plan to run away—although some of the dates would end in tears, just to make it realistic.

Gradually Michael Manning faded into the background of these stories, and we focused solely on Madison, who was having an elaborate and exciting life in New York, where she was landing dream jobs at glossy magazines and dating famous men who were artists and poets and photographers. Madison briefly had a drug habit, but she kicked it in the nick of time before it destroyed her life.

She vowed to never settle down and rarely thought of Michael Manning and his small world—where it seemed his purpose in life was to please his parents, which was why she had left him in the first place.

THE PEOPLE SKIRT

The people skirt was a pencil skirt that had black-and-white drawings of people printed on it. It was cotton and form-fitting. It was a skirt for skinny people. I wasn't skinny.

The people skirt cost fifty dollars. I wanted the people skirt for many months but couldn't get it because I was having a jaw operation. After the operation, where I lost so much blood I had to have two blood transfusions, I lost a lot of weight so I was able to fit into the people skirt. I wore a yellow tank top with the people skirt. They wired my jaw shut for six weeks, and I could only drink instead of eat. And I couldn't really talk or yell or scream because my jaw was wired shut.

My mother told me nice girls don't walk and smoke. They don't wear short skirts and Doc Martens and motorcycle jackets because it's not feminine. She did not tell me about the people skirt. Player's cigarettes are for men. She did not say anything about the people skirt, which was form-fitting. "If you get pregnant, get an abortion," she said. But she was really talking about herself and what she would have done if abortion had been legal.

This is why when I walked through the empty parking lot toward the library and got catcalled by some men on their lunch break, I was taken aback. I had never been addressed this way before. Like a woman.

I'm fifteen, I wanted to shout to shame them the way they had shamed me. But I didn't because I couldn't because my jaw was wired shut.

POPULARITY

All through Grade 6 and most of Grade 7, I didn't have any friends to hang out with at school because my only school friend moved away. I had no gym partner and no one to talk to between classes or on breaks.

Every recess, I made my way to the primary wing of the school and sat in one of the bathroom stalls until the fifteen-minute break was up.

In the spring of Grade 7, our gym teacher made us all try out for the track and field team. The schoolyard was turned into an obstacle course. We were timed doing such things as short-metre races, high jumps, and hurdles.

I was pretty much terrible at every sport except the sprints and short races, where my running times were among the best in the class, so I was placed on the relay team with two other girls and a popular rich girl, Alyssa.

We had to attend after-school practices to prepare for a city-wide elementary competition at a local high school. The four of us ended up spending a lot of time together. On the day of the competition, we sat in the bleachers for hours, waiting for our race.

Alyssa and I hit it off because it turned out we had the same sense of humour, so we spent most of our time laughing, writing notes to each other, and making inside jokes that undoubtedly caused the other two girls to feel excluded.

After the race, where we came in second place, I was shocked when Alyssa called and asked if I wanted to hang out. I agreed but was skeptical, because I had no friends and she was popular.

Once our friendship was sealed, Alyssa decided I needed

a complete makeover before we entered Grade 8. She told me what to wear and what name brands to buy—much to the dismay of my mother, who could not afford for me to have a closet full of Ralph Lauren shirts.

Alyssa told me how to act and how to wear my hair until I was eventually accepted into her friend group, but I knew I always teetered on the edge, a tagalong.

Alyssa could mould me any way she liked. To win her favour, I was willing to do anything she said.

She would defend me to anyone who dared bully me yet seemed to enjoy humiliating me in front of others.

A favourite pastime of hers was to tell me that guys who did not like me had crushes on me until she got my hopes up.

She would say things like "You shouldn't wear your hair over your eye because if you end up making out with someone, it will freak them out when they see it."

She would be cruel, and when I pulled away, she would draw me back in by telling me secrets or being unbelievably kind.

Other kids were beginning to accept me as well. I was invited to parties, and once I was even invited to a concert with a group of her friends when Alyssa was out of town.

I got the feeling she didn't like this.

* * *

On the Grade 8 school trip to Quebec City and Montreal, Alyssa decided to turn everyone against me.

We had been looking forward to this trip all year. We talked for hours about all the things we would do and all the fun we would have. We hoped we could go shopping in Montreal. We looked forward to getting to stay in a hotel.

When I was unpacking in the hotel room, she saw I had the same designer underwear that she wore. It was a birthday present from my sister, but Alyssa accused me of copying her. In this world, copying someone was a sin worse than murder.

This breach resulted in her not speaking to me for the entire trip.

Not only did she not speak to me, but also she told her boyfriend who then told all of his friends who then told everyone else, and once again I was demoted to an undesirable to whom no one would speak unless they were making fun of my underwear.

I sat by myself during meals, and in our free time, I just went back to the hotel room and watched TV.

When we got back home after the trip, Alyssa acted like none of it had happened. It was as if she had just created the rift to enjoy watching me suffer, like someone who tortures animals for kicks.

"Wasn't that fun?" she said as we got off the school bus, and then, "Let's hang out this weekend."

And of course we did.

I'M TAKING CARE OF IT

On the last day of Grade 8, I walked out of the girls' washroom and into the hall, where I found two boys laughing hysterically. *Hysterically* is an understatement. One was near tears, the other having an asthma attack.

"What is wrong with you?" I asked.

They were laughing so hard they couldn't speak and pointed at a tall loner girl named Geneviève who had a splotch of blood on her white track pants. She walked into the history classroom—our final class of the day—seemingly unaware of her situation.

"Grow up," I said, but my response only made them laugh more.

Alyssa came up to us and wanted to know what was going on.

"Maybe she doesn't know," Alyssa said.

"We should tell her," I said.

"God, how embarrassing," Alyssa gasped.

Alyssa and I decided to offer her a pair of shorts or a jacket to put around her waist and hide the stain. Alyssa suggested we could take her to the school nurse to get a pad.

Geneviève had moved the year before from Quebec with her mother and younger brother after (it was rumoured) her father had died. Occasionally someone would mimic her accent, but generally she talked to no one, and no one talked to her, which made the taunting even crueller.

What was happening to Geneviève was just about my worst nightmare and likely the worst nightmare of every bleeder in that class.

While we were conspiring on what to do, news spread about Geneviève's bloodstain, and more kids were whispering and laughing behind her back.

Geneviève was seated at her desk, reading. If she knew she was the butt of a joke, she didn't let on.

"Hi," Alyssa said as we approached Geneviève's desk.

"Hi," Geneviève said coolly.

"I think you have your period," Alyssa said bluntly. "It's like on the back of your pants." She laughed in a commiserating way.

"I know," Geneviève said casually.

"Do you want a pad or a sweater to cover up?" I asked.

"I've got some extra gym shorts," Alyssa offered.

We were tripping over ourselves to come to Geneviève's rescue, not out of any great care for Geneviève herself—we didn't really know her—but because Geneviève's shame was our own.

For those of us who bled, the trick to surviving was to ensure that bleeding was neither talked about nor seen, which was why the boys seeing Geneviève's blood sent them into a fit.

"No thanks," Geneviève said.

"Are you sure?" I asked. I was shocked—even a little insulted—that she didn't want our help.

"I'm taking care of it," she said.

Confused, we took our seats.

When the teacher began his lesson, I couldn't concentrate because all I could think of was Geneviève free-bleeding at her seat.

Giggles erupted in waves, and when the teacher noticed he demanded to know what was so funny, but no one dared tell.

After a long silence, he continued his lesson despite the strange energy in the room, which he likely chalked up to it being the last day of school.

At the end of class, all eyes turned to Geneviève, including mine. I was seated two rows over, behind her.

Geneviève put her books away slowly and tidied up her desk. I did the same, hoping like the others to get a glance at the back of her track pants. I had gone from helper to spectator and now I wanted to see the show.

When she finally stood up, I was surprised and relieved for Geneviève that the bloodstain had not grown all that much. It was darker now, having dried a little, and looked more like a chocolate ice cream stain than blood.

No one spoke as Geneviève walked across the room and out the door. Her posture was straight, head high, cheeks unflushed.

She appeared to carry no shame. No embarrassment.

She walked at an ordinary pace, holding her book under her arm.

Geneviève lived farther away from the school than most of the kids, so we all trailed along slowly behind her. She kept the pace and we followed.

At first the taunting continued, but eventually because she appeared so unbothered by the attention, the kids who were making fun of her grew bored and started picking on each other instead.

As quickly as Geneviève's blood had entered all our psyches, it left.

BARN BASH

On the edge of town, a large mall was being constructed beside an old field and a barn. Almost every weekend, kids from different high schools threw wild parties there, and sometimes fights would break out.

I had heard of barn bashes but had never gone to one until the summer between Grade 9 and 10, when Alyssa and I decided we would go.

We pre-drank at her boyfriend Pete's house. He lived in one of the new subdivisions near the mall with the monster houses, a barren neighbourhood with no trees, just saplings. We drank most of the bottle of sherry Alyssa stole from her mother and the bottle of vodka I stole from mine.

By the time we headed for the barn bash, Alyssa and I were staggering. She hung off Pete as we walked along the road and through the field to the rotting barn, which, according to rumours, would soon be demolished.

His friends, thinking we were both out of it, started making fun of Alyssa's tits, and Pete didn't defend her. He just laughed along.

I slurred, "You guys are assholes." But they either didn't hear me or pretended not to.

When we got to the party, there were about 150 kids from at least three neighbouring high schools—groups of kids who didn't normally hang out with each other were partying and having fun sharing booze and smokes and food. I recognized some from our school, but they were the type who only talked to me if I was with Alyssa.

Alyssa and Pete said they were checking out the extension

on the mall and would be back soon. I asked Alyssa if she was all right. I'd never seen her so drunk before.

She said she was fine but that I couldn't go with them because she and Pete needed to talk about their relationship.

"But don't leave without me, because you're staying over tonight," she said. Her parents were away, so we had no curfew. She handed me the rest of the sherry bottle and left with Pete.

I sat down on an old tree stump and watched the party. I was so drunk that I was unbothered sitting alone. Some kids were smoking up, others fucking, some were trying to set the barn on fire while another group tried to stop them for fear of the party being shut down.

"Don't wreck this for everyone," a girl said.

A couple of people attempted to talk to me, but I was all slurs.

One guy came over and started grabbing at me. I tried to push him off, but he would not leave me alone. Every time I shut my eyes, everything spun, and when I opened them, he was still on top of me.

At some point skinheads showed up with baseball bats, screaming racist, anti-Semitic, and homophobic slurs.

A fight broke out.

Kids were screaming.

I could smell smoke but didn't realize it was the barn until it went up in flames.

There were sirens and flashlights.

Kids ran every which way, including me, but I fell down immediately because my pants were at my ankles.

Someone helped me up, and then I pulled up my jeans and ran as fast as could, which was pretty fast, despite my condition.

At the road, I saw the kids from my school and one kid from church pile into a car. When I asked if I could get a ride too, they said there wasn't room and drove away, leaving me alone at the edge of town, where there were no pay phones.

I held my bus pass tightly and headed for the nearest stop, about twenty minutes away. As soon as I started walking, I began to see double. I held up one finger and saw two. I looked at my feet and there were four.

I had to be careful to neither stagger into the woods nor veer out onto the road and get hit by a car, but it was impossible to walk forward in my state, and I fell down after each attempt, skinning my knees and hands on the gravel.

I decided to crawl. If a car drove by, I would lie down flat so they wouldn't see me, and I made my way like this until I reached the bus stop.

Once I got there, I collapsed and passed out.

Out of some kind of bizarre coincidence, a girl a grade older than me, who my sister used to babysit, was being driven home by a friend when she saw me at the side of the road.

She and her friend hauled me into the car. The drive would have been humiliating except I was too drunk to feel shame, the one good thing about being obliterated. I told her I was staying at Alyssa's house, and fortunately she knew the address because I couldn't remember it.

I knocked on Alyssa's door, but no one answered, so I sat on the steps and passed out for the second time that night.

When I awoke, it was morning. Alyssa was standing in front of me covered in black hickeys.

My bus pass was on the ground in front of me.

I had vomited on it.

"I was so worried about you," Alyssa said. "We were looking for you all night."

"I'm sure," I said, standing up unsteadily because I was still drunk.

When I got home, my underwear had blood in it and there were bruises on my thighs, neither of which I told anyone about.

SKIPPING

You believe you are ugly. You have been ugly all your life. You wear sunglasses whenever you can so no one sees your face. You were born with a lazy eye and the surgeries opened it but made you disfigured. They made your eye not quite close all the way and peak like a triangle. The kids in elementary school called you Popeye. Clever actually. By the time your mother found a good doctor, the specialist, there was nothing that could be done.

Ever since you could remember, adults had asked your parents about your eye, and kids at school found new ways each year to let you know just how disgusting they thought you were. So you tried to look normal by wearing your hair over your eye. You realized that you would rather have people wonder why your hair was over your eye than actually see your eye. You try to imagine what it would be like to walk around in life and not be ashamed of your face.

You know that feeling when you decide to skip school and meet your boyfriend, your relatively new boyfriend, downtown at the mall. It's March and you've been dating since February. And he's really cute. He's bad for you, but you won't realize this for four years. So right now there's this cute boy waiting for you at the Galleria, and you're going record shopping.

You get off the 6 Richmond bus and walk down Dundas toward the mall. It's before 9:00 a.m. and the sky is bright and hopeful and the air is cool. You can see your breath. You didn't bring mittens or a scarf. You never wear a hat. Your pea coat is open and the air makes you shiver. All you can think about is having a cigarette, so you go into the variety store and buy a pack and light one up and look around at the empty streets.

Some people are going to work, but most of the stores haven't even opened yet.

Everything feels quiet and settled. You don't know it right in this moment, but you're going to skip school for the next two weeks because your mother will go on a bender and you'll want to get back at her the only way you know how. You will be suspended for another two weeks by the guidance counsellor who had contracted polio as a child. One of his arms is smaller than the other. You won't feel sorry for him because he's mean, and he reminds you of yourself more than you care to admit. But right now this feeling of freedom is addictive. You want it to last the same way you want your cigarette to last.

You make your way to the mall, where your boyfriend is waiting for you. He has headphones on and is probably listening to his favourite band, which is now your favourite band. He wears a leather motorcycle jacket, and as you walk toward him you can't believe that someone who looks like him wants to be with someone who looks like you.

Not now, but in a year, he will be one of the three people in your life permitted to see you without makeup and without the hair in your face. He'll also be the first person you fuck and the first person who hits you and you hit back. But not today.

Today you spend an hour getting ready and covering your eyes in black makeup and you straighten your bangs with an iron so they cover your face in just the right way. And then you put your sunglasses on, and you board the 6 Richmond bus.

Today your favourite bus driver, Big Dave, is driving. Big Dave who cracks jokes and sings and chats up just about everyone, making the ride pleasant for even the most miserable among us.

SIT DOWN BESIDE MEGAN

Do you know what is boring? Do you know what is really fucking boring?

Watching your high school boyfriend practise with his hard-core band in the basement of his mother's hair salon. Your boyfriend plays bass and you think to yourself, why would anyone want to play bass? If I were in a band—if I had any musical talent whatsoever—I would probably want to play guitar or be the lead singer. But I guess they already have a guitar player and lead singer. Mick. Mick with the green hair and ripped black jeans and safety pins in his ears. Mick calls smoke breaks when he feels like it and everyone goes along and doesn't ask for a smoke break until he says they can have one.

I'm getting the feeling my boyfriend is just in the band so the band can have a place to practise. He wasn't in the band before. He's the newest member, and he and Mick weren't even friends before. I don't think Mick even knew my boyfriend existed. They just sat near each other in math. I'm sure it's not a coincidence that my boyfriend's mother's hair salon is the perfect place to practise since Mick just got kicked out of the house and they can't practise at his dad's place anymore. Now Mick squats at the vacant building downtown or he stays at Megan's house—his silent but faithfully devoted girlfriend.

My boyfriend asked if I would come and watch them practise because Megan always comes to watch Mick. Megan, with her brown bobbed hair and frosted pink lipstick, sits in the corner and watches them as if she's really fucking interested. She stares so intently at her boyfriend, she hardly blinks.

How could she be so fucking interested? They are terrible. They are a terrible band. Okay, I admit I'm not a hardcore fan to begin with, but this band doesn't even know what they are doing. They don't know how to act or practise. Mick doesn't seem to even know how to tune his guitar. Every time they start playing, Mick says something doesn't sound right, and the drummer says, "You need to tune your guitar," and Mick says, "It's not that," and they go on like this for what seems like hours.

In an attempt to relieve my boredom, I try to start a conversation with Megan. We're the girlfriends. We're the girlfriends; therefore, we don't exist unless they want one of us to run upstairs and get something like a beer or chips or a pick. I think this would be more fun if I was on acid or if I had some weed or if Megan had any kind of personality that I could work with. She just sits there staring. If I ask her a question, she gives me these one-word answers.

"What school do you go to?" I ask.

"Beal," she says.

"I go to Beal too. Are you in the art program?" I ask.

"No," she says.

"What grade you are in?"

"Ten," she says.

Okay then. I'll just fuck off over here to the other side of the room and let you continue to stare at your boyfriend.

Mick starts to get really testy with the bandmates. He wrote a song and apparently no one plays it right. No one understands his artistic intentions. But the song is pretty terrible, if you ask me.

My boyfriend can tell I'm pissed. I'm trying not to let my feelings show on my face, but that's pretty much near impossible for me. I can't be fake and I can't lie, and when something is wrong everyone can tell by the look on my face. My boyfriend catches me rolling my eyes at something Mick says and he mouths, *Don't*. He has a kind of panicked look like he's afraid of what I will say or do next or maybe he's afraid of what Mick will do. I'm not sure.

There will not be a repeat performance of this, I can assure you. I will not be a prop. I thought it might be interesting to hear them play before I realized they were using my boyfriend, but now it's unbearable to watch the drama unfold. My boyfriend is just sitting on the couch with his bass in his hands, pretending to tune it or something. They call him in for one song and then as soon as he starts playing, Mick says, "No, no, no, no... Don't you even listen to our music?"

"Sorry, man," is all my boyfriend mutters, and sits back down. Weak. He's a weak bitch, my boyfriend. He doesn't like confrontation. Doesn't care if he wins a fight. Do you know how frustrating it is to fight with someone who won't fight back? He'll take the road of least conflict, even if it takes him nowhere, even if he ends up going in circles. And he'll defer to whoever has the more dominant personality—his mother, his sister, me, Mick. While I don't want him running around beating everyone up like my dad did in high school, it would be nice if he stood up for himself once in a while. I mean, who joins a band and then doesn't even get to play?

I would tell Mick to fuck off myself, but I'm not certain Mick is the type of guy who draws the line at hitting a girl. There have been rumours about Mick. He was at the centre of a big fight after school where about three kids were hospitalized and ten got suspended. I can usually tell how far to push with someone. Like my father, for instance. He can yell and topple tables and throw books across the room, but I know he's never going to hit me, so I always fight back.

At one point while Mick and the other guys are conferring in the middle of the room, and my boyfriend is back on the couch like a punished child, I guess I let out a big sigh and then stretch my leg, knocking over a beer bottle. I don't mean to do it. I don't mean to draw attention to myself like that, but Mick hears it and stops talking and looks over at me. He's got a mean face.

"Excuse me," he says.

Everyone in the band looks at me except my boyfriend, who keeps his eyes on his bass; he's frozen, not wanting to look at me, not wanting to look at Mick. Even Megan looks my way, like she's seeing me in the room for the first time since we got here.

"Everything cool?" he asks.

It's a horrible situation. I've drawn attention to myself in the worst way possible and all I want to do is laugh.

I want to say something that could cause a shit show, but instead I just say quickly, "Yep, everything's cool. Sorry."

Mick doesn't acknowledge that I've spoken to him, and he turns his back to me and directs the band to start (finally) playing. He even has my boyfriend get in on this song.

Apparently, the song is for Megan, and it's about the time they almost broke up because she was pregnant and had an abortion. Then they got back together. Mick recounts the story to everyone in the room like he's talking about a vacation they went on and not one of their most painful, private moments.

Mick starts talking to everyone super nice. He even says a few nice things to Megan, who smiles like she's been touched by a god.

I think to myself, I'm not sure how much longer I can take all this.

And then they play and they play and they play. And the music is terrible and my ears are ringing and there's a musty smell in the room that is suddenly making me feel like I want to throw up, so I get up, cross the room, and start to head up the stairs to the salon, where I can twirl in the stylist chairs and maybe run a brush through my hair or smell the shampoos.

As I climb a few steps, Mick stops the song he's playing and says to me, "Hey, where you going?"

"Upstairs," I say, and take another step.

"We're in the middle of a song. You can't walk out in the middle of a song." He laughs in this exasperated but sort of lighthearted way that sounds like he's being friendly, but he's actually being the opposite of friendly.

"I just wanted to get a drink of water," I say, curling my hand around the metal handrail. My hand is damp and the metal cools my skin.

"Sit back down," Mick says, as if he's talking to an unruly puppy. "Sit back down beside Megan."

The air in the room is suddenly stale and hot. The bandmates are looking at the floor and so is Megan, but this time my boyfriend is looking at me. He's looking right at me and not saying a fucking thing. But he doesn't have to because I know what he wants. He wants me to shut the fuck up and sit by Megan. He wants me to sit there until we're told by Mick that we can leave. Sit there like a good girl. Like a girlfriend whose job it is to watch her boyfriend play in a shitty band.

My body temperature goes from hot to burning. My face is red. My temples are throbbing. I clutch the handrail tighter, and the dampness from my hand causes my grip to slip. My legs are shaky and feel like they won't hold me up anymore. I know I could save this moment. I know in one move I could dissolve all the tension in the room and the band will go on playing and everyone will pretend none of this happened—especially my boyfriend.

I stare at Mick directly in his eyes as if I am clear about what he is and isn't capable of doing—even though I have no fucking idea.

"Sit down," he says again firmly.

In another universe my boyfriend would step in and tell

Mick to fuck off and kick everyone out of his mother's salon or the bandmates would stand up to their leader or even Megan would come to my defence in some form of solidarity or, in this other, better, more perfect universe that doesn't seem like it can or will ever exist, I would turn my back on Mick's request, continue walking up the stairs, and go home.

But none of this happens.

Instead, I avert my eyes like the others and quietly say, "Okay."

Then I release my grip on the handrail and walk back down the few steps I had managed to climb, and I go and sit down right the fuck beside Megan.

Mick nods, then shoots me a half-smile.

Megan and I sit in the same position—knees bent with our arms wrapped around them in a hug.

The band starts playing.

Megan nods along to the music. I sit very still, trying to maintain a neutral expression on my face.

Although the tension in the room seems to have disappeared, somehow it finds its way directly into my body—my hands tremble and my heart beats faster than I thought it could.

"Your boyfriend is an asshole," I say to Megan without looking at her.

"I know," she says.

JACKIE GLEASON

My father was always angling, always trying to get something for nothing or something for cheap. At restaurants, he'd sneak in airplane bottles of booze in his trouser pockets, order a pop, and when the server had her back turned, he'd spike his drink with rum. A relationship with his daughter could be turned into a maid service for twenty dollars a week. He paid me to clean his one-bedroom apartment—the rundown white building with the outdoor pool beside White Oaks Mall. It was across the city from where I lived and took an hour by bus to get there after school. There was a Hasty Market beside the building, and I would buy a bag of sour-cream-and-onion chips before letting myself into his apartment.

The place was easy to clean; I just had to vacuum, change his sheets, dust, and scrub the bathroom. Having recently left the woman he'd left my mother for, my father didn't have very much in the way of worldly possessions. All furniture was utilitarian: a bed, a couch, an end table, a kitchen table, chairs. There was no art on the wall, no books. Everything was beige. The only trace of an interest was the golf magazines in the bathroom and the tees and balls absent-mindedly left on his dresser top with his pocket change. While I cleaned, he made spaghetti or ordered pizza.

He'd say, "I'm not going to ask you about school," and then he didn't bother to ask me anything at all. We ate side by side on the couch, watching *The Andy Griffith Show*, then *The Honeymooners*, on his old black-and-white TV. The shows made him laugh until tears formed in his eyes.

But I wasn't laughing, so he'd explain each joke after it was delivered, trying to make me see Jackie Gleason's goddamn genius, his bloody brilliance.

THE FIGHT

My boyfriend and I got into a fight and he pushed me into the bathroom door—so hard it felt like I'd been hit with a baseball.

I pushed him back and ran out of the house while he shouted my name over and over so loud I was sure all the neighbours could hear.

I ran for three solid blocks and stopped at a phone booth near the pharmacy to catch my breath.

When I realized I hadn't brought cigarettes, my chest tightened and the pang of regret was so bottomless it felt like I'd jumped from a high bridge. So I called my mother's house collect and he answered. He was still there. I imagined him sitting on my mother's yellow couch, finishing the potato chips and dip we had planned to eat while watching the movie we'd rented from the video store. I wasn't hungry anymore, but I would kill for a cigarette.

"You beat me," I said into the phone. I liked the way it sounded when the words came out of my mouth because it gave me the upper hand and it made me feel pretty, like a sad girl on a talk show—until it occurred to me that he really did beat me and now I knew exactly what he was capable of, exactly what I was in for.

MEANING OF THE UNIVERSE

I discovered the meaning of the universe on my first acid trip, when I was sixteen. I was visiting Thea in her new town where she and her parents had just moved: Guelph, Ontario—the home of John McCrae, the physician who wrote the poem "In Flanders Fields," a poem we had to memorize in Mrs. Brown's fourth-grade class. I was no good at memorization. I was no good at school, and this was the poem that made me hate poetry.

The acid was called Purple Double Barrel.

We were in the food court of the mall downtown.

I said to Thea and her new friend Stephanie, who dressed like Cleopatra and acted like she knew Thea better than me: "You guys are peer-pressuring me. Like in an afterschool special."

"You don't have to do it," Thea said. She knew I was afraid. "It just would be more fun if you did. Then we'd all be on acid."

The pill was so tiny. Much smaller than my birth control pills. I held it in the palm of my hand and stared at it and thought, I'm going to be the type of person who does acid.

I was not the type of person who did cocaine because my mother told me I could get a heart attack from cocaine. But my mother knew nothing about acid. She was too old to be a hippie and had not experimented with anything other than alcohol.

When Thea and I were little, Thea was an avid reader and had read about "angel dust" in one of her library books. One day we were in my basement pretending we were on angel dust and seeing colours and crystals and pretty things all over the damp and dark cellar that smelled of mice and still held my father's old *Playboy* magazines tucked away in some corner, along with the handgun he used to shoot bullets at tin cans.

Now here I was holding Purple Double Barrel in my hand like it was a four-leaf clover.

To say the acid trip was good would be an understatement. It was beyond description.

It made me feel like I was a balloon.

On this acid trip, I believed I had discovered the meaning of the universe. I pitied all of those who didn't understand. I pitied all the people with miserable lives, like my parents.

The acid trip also made me forget the twinge of jealousy I felt toward all the cool friends Thea made at her new high school, especially her friendship with Stephanie. It made me forget about my terrible boyfriend and my mom who was drunk all the time and how badly I was doing in school and how much I hated my drama teacher who gave me a C because I couldn't do an Italian accent. The acid made me feel smart and light and intellectual.

After traipsing around Guelph for hours—in parks, cemeteries, churches, trying to recite "In Flanders Fields"—we finally ended up at Thea's house. Her parents and sister were asleep. We made bagels and cream cheese and snuck down to her room, where we listened to the same song over again in the dark, on an album she took from her parents' record collection. Her parents didn't do drugs, but they were real hippies. We thought the song was sending us messages.

This is where the meaning-of-the-universe moment comes in. We lay on Thea's floor side by side holding hands when I— yes, it was me—discovered the meaning of the universe. Not just the meaning of life but the universe. In one moment I knew nothing, and in the next I knew everything.

Once I explained it to Thea, she knew it too, and we both cried out of relief and happiness, knowing that we would not be searching for this for our entire lives. We decided not to tell anyone because we didn't think they could handle this epic truth.

When we woke up the next morning, the meaning of the universe became a faded memory, a dream, and all we were left with was a bad stomach ache that Stephanie told us was gut rot caused by the rat poison they cut the acid with.

BORN AGAIN

One day I woke up and all my high school friends became born-again Christians. I had gone away with my dad for two weeks, and when I returned everyone had converted. No one drank or smoked or did drugs or fucked. No one partied or stayed out late. All they did was talk about church or try to get me to go to church with them.

We were seventeen, heading into Grade 11. Until then, all my friends were the opposite of born-again Christians. They partied, and I was the square in the group.

When you were around them you had no idea what was going to happen next. And the drama. There was so much drama. They were always obsessing about guys, dating guys, breaking up with guys.

At first, I thought it was a joke, so I quizzed them: "What do you mean you believe in God?"

"We believe in God," they said, "and we think you should too—or you're going to hell."

Kit was my closest friend in the group. She was also hilarious. We were paired to work on a project in French class, and we met at the university library to work on it, hoping we could find some cute guys to stare at. Kit was boy-crazy.

Before we even set down to work, Kit let out a big fart that smelled like eggs, and we both laughed until we pissed ourselves. Kit actually pissed her pants right in the middle of the library.

We weren't even high. That fart and her peeing her pants sealed our friendship, and we hung out every day after that. We never did hand in the project, and we both failed the class.

It wasn't just Kit who converted but our two other friends, Farah and Tammy.

"But why?" I asked Farah.

"Because God is love," she said. Farah's dad was born in Haiti and became a self-described ex-Catholic when he came to Canada, and her mother who lived in Quebec City most of her life was atheist.

Farah and I bonded because neither of us had been baptized as children, unlike everyone else we knew—although I eventually got baptized then confirmed through the United Church when I was twelve during a very brief religious phase of my own.

But even during this phase I never believed in God. My dad bashed the Catholic Church every chance he got for as long as I could remember because the Church and Catholic school ruined his childhood. My mother grew up in the United Church, and despite my grandmother being devout, my mother wasn't a practising Christian.

Kit never knew her father, but her mother who had grown up on a farm near Ottawa had turned her back on religion during her hippie phase and now belonged to the Unitarian Fellowship. Kit's mother was also studying Buddhism and dabbled in spiritualism. Kit had been baptized but only at her grandmother's insistence.

Tammy was the biggest partier of all. She was the one who always found a way to get booze and drugs for all of us. I don't know how she did it, but every weekend she never showed up empty-handed. If you couldn't get anything, Tammy always had more than enough and was willing to share. She was a tall girl who didn't take shit from anyone. She had rebelled against her parents who were Dutch Reform, and I couldn't understand why she wanted to be born again.

"My parents and I are getting along now. They're so happy for me," Tammy said.

I wasn't friends with the rest of the kids who got converted, but these three—Kit, Farah, and Tammy—were my friend group. I loved them more than I loved my own family. They were the friends I spent lunches and spare periods smoking with in the coffee shop, figuring out what party we would go to or how we could get into bars underage.

When I was with these girls, I wanted to forget my home life existed. I got wrapped up in all their problems, so I didn't have to think about my own.

Finding out all my friends were born-again Christians caused my world to close in on me. I couldn't relate to them as they talked about a sermon where everyone was speaking in tongues. Or when they all got tickets for a Christian rock concert and didn't invite me. They said I wouldn't like the band because I didn't believe in God.

I had nowhere to go on weeknights when I couldn't stand the sight of my mother. Normally Kit and I would spend hours at doughnut shops or drive out to the country and look at the stars and the city.

My entire reason for existing vanished, yet I would not be converted.

* * *

Farah was the one who finally told me how the conversion went down. In the two weeks that I had been away, a friend of a friend invited Kit, Farah, and Tammy to the church for a weekend festival where they had rented fair games and rides, had ongoing sermons, children and youth activities, and an outreach program to onboard teen girls into the youth group.

My friends initially went as a joke. They thought it would be funny to get high and hang out with a bunch of Christians. They all took acid and went to the festival.

Kit got lured in because she had the hots for the youth

pastor who told a story about being a drug dealer and turning his life around.

Farah said she felt the spirit of Jesus like on TV—although she didn't tell her parents she was born again because she didn't think they would approve.

And Tammy, who carried an enormous amount of guilt for letting her parents down, said, "Believing in God helped ease that guilt."

So by the time I returned to town, the church had its hooks into all of them. They had volunteered at the church every day since the festival. And all of them had quit smoking, given up drugs, alcohol, and sex, and made a promise to God.

While Farah and Tammy drifted away from me, Kit held on strong to our friendship because she wanted to save me.

"If you don't convert, you're going to hell," she said daily. She'd shake her head when I lit a cigarette and sigh when I asked if we were ever going to drink together again. I would try to talk about all the fun we used to have, and she would put up her hand to stop me.

* * *

One evening she called me up and asked if I wanted to go to Reggie's, a restaurant downtown.

We ordered coffee and sat at the back in the smoking section near the pay phones. I was surprised when she didn't complain or roll her eyes. It was around 7:30 p.m. and not too busy.

There was a bus driver in his uniform across from us, reading a paper. The radio was on, playing something from the Top 40. An old tube TV hung precariously on the wall near the washrooms. The teen employees chatted among themselves by the cash register, flirting meanly with one another.

Being with Kit felt different now. There was a weird tension between us that made me tired. It used to be so easy and fun. We strained to find topics of conversation we would both enjoy. If I talked about the old days (as in two months ago), Kit would get a pained look in her eyes. And when she talked about the church, I would look away and pretend I was distracted by something else.

All Kit wanted to do was talk about Pastor Rick, who she was now dating.

"Isn't it frowned upon to date the youth pastor?" I asked.

"No," she said a little defensively. "It's not like we're going to have sex or anything. Actually, he's a little mad at me that I'm not a virgin."

"How did he find out?" I asked.

"Youth group," she said. "It's where we confess things."

"Maybe he'll break up with you," I said cheerily. "Tell him more."

"Fuck you," Kit said, then quickly looked up. "Sorry."

"You think God is listening to you say 'fuck'?" I asked.

"Yes," she said.

"He must be very bored if he's got time to do that." I lit a cigarette and blew it in Kit's face.

"Gimme a drag of that thing. I'm having a nic fit."

"I thought you wanted to quit," I said.

She took a drag of my cigarette.

"Won't God be mad at you?" I asked.

"I'll be praying tomorrow. Actually, maybe I better pray now," she said, and looked up. "Dear Lord..." She looked at me. "Here's what I don't get—do I pray to God or Jesus?"

"Ask Pastor Rick."

"I feel like it's something I should know."

"I don't think it matters. Just do whatever you feel like," I said.

"Dear God and/or Jesus, please forgive me for my sin of smoking and cursing."

"I don't think God cares if you smoke. He's got bigger fish to fry, like world hunger and acid rain," I said. "Why don't you ask God to fix the ozone layer? Sometimes I'm so worried about it, I can't sleep at night."

"When the world ends, only God's chosen will be saved. Everyone else will be sent to hell," Kit said.

"What about people of other religions?"

She shrugged. "They really just have to be Christians."

"Even your mother?" I asked.

Kit nodded.

"Don't you think it's weird that you call your boyfriend Pastor Rick? Like can't you just call him Rick?"

Kit laughed. "I could... I just wish you would come to the youth group one time. Please, please, please."

"No way," I said.

"When the world ends, I'm going to heaven. God loves me. And he loves you too, if you'll let him."

"I've been baptized. So I'm not going to hell. I'm good," I said.

"Pastor Rick says you need to be born again and accept Jesus into your heart as your personal saviour. That's the only ticket to Heaven."

Across the restaurant, I noticed a woman staring at me. I put my hair in front of my eye, and Kit brushed the hair out of my face.

"Don't do that," she said.

"It makes me comfortable," I said.

"You shouldn't be ashamed of who you are."

"Easy for you to say. You don't know what it's like to be ugly," I said.

"You're beautiful and you're my best friend. That's why I

want you to meet Pastor Rick so bad. I want him to help you with all your problems."

"Don't tell him about me. I don't want his help. And don't tell him about my mom."

* * *

Kit suggested we go to the mall and get some fries, and on the way, we stopped at an arcade so I could play video games.

While I played, Kit kept looking at her watch. She seemed edgy and impatient. I asked if she wanted to play, but she shook her head no.

"Satan?" I asked.

"Let's go," she said.

On the way out, a guy asked if we wanted pot. I said yes and Kit said no. I only had eight dollars, so I asked her to lend me two, which she did reluctantly if I promised we could go to the mall and get fries.

"It's really skid to buy drugs at an arcade," she said.

"I'm desperate. I'm my only fun these days." I stopped to roll a joint.

"Pastor Rick thinks you're going to lead me down a Satan path. You're Eve and I'm Adam, and I'm not strong enough to resist you. For instance, when you light that joint, I'm going to have to have some. And I've been so good while you were away with your dad."

"Oh, so you don't want me around?" I asked.

"I want you to be part of the youth group too. Then we can hang out all the time and watch out for each other. Maybe you'll find a boyfriend who you don't fight with so much."

"So now my boyfriend is shitty too? Maybe I'm going to go home after this," I said.

"No, no, please don't go home. I'm sorry. I shouldn't have

said all that stuff. Let's just go to the food court and hang out like we always do."

I lit the joint and took a drag and then Kit took a drag too. Once inside the mall, I stepped in a large puddle at the bottom of the stairs.

My right foot was soaked. Kit laughed with me, and for a moment it was just like old times.

The food court was empty except for a woman in a white coat eating alone and a security guard who was chatting up the teen girls who work at the fish-and-chips place.

I told Kit she looked stoned and she began to get paranoid. "I need to look normal," she said.

"Did you ever think that Pastor Rick doesn't have sex because he can't get it up or something?"

Kit laughed. "No, I've felt his hard-on."

"When?" I asked.

"When we're making out. He sort of humps me."

We started to laugh. Kit ordered some fries and we shared them.

Kit looked at her watch, then suddenly became serious. "Let's calm down."

"I am calm. I'm high but also calm," I laughed, and squirted ketchup onto a napkin while Kit clasped her hands together and started to pray.

She stopped and looked up at me. "It's rude to not pray with someone who is praying," Kit said.

"I don't pray."

Kit crossed herself, then ate a fry.

"Isn't crossing yourself Catholic?" I asked.

"I don't know," she said.

"I don't think born agains cross themselves."

"For someone who is determined to hate religion, you sure have a lot of information," Kit said.

"My dad's Catholic," I said.

Kit's face brightened, and I turned around to find Pastor Rick looming over the table in acid-washed jeans and a baggy black shirt—tucked in.

Kit jumped up and gave him a hug like a fan girl. "I've wanted you two to meet so badly."

I glared at Kit. "Did you plan this?"

She smiled a little.

"You didn't know I was coming?" he asked.

I shook my head.

"I thought she wouldn't come if I told her," Kit said.

Pastor Rick looked at Kit's eyes. "Are you high?" he asked.

Kit cannot lie. "It was for a good cause," she said. "To bring you two together."

I stared at her in disbelief.

"Kit is very worried about you," Pastor Rick said.

"She doesn't need to worry," I said. "I'm good. I'm really fucking good." I glared at Kit.

"I hope you don't mind, but Kit shared a few things about you with me."

I mouthed, *I hate you*, to Kit but she looked away.

"Kit told me about your mother and that you drink and smoke a lot of pot."

"Did you tell Pastor Rick that you do acid every weekend?"

Pastor Rick looked at Kit.

"Used to. Acid's bad. Very bad," she said.

"She also says you skip school and that you get into fights with your boyfriend. Is that right?"

"That is private stuff I told Kit in private. She is or was my best friend."

"She is your friend. That's why she's so worried about you and the path you're taking."

"I'm fine. And actually I do go to school."

"Kit said you were molested," he said.

"What the fuck, Kit?"

Pastor Rick lifted his hands. "Kit thinks you need help. I'm here to help."

Pastor Rick had a soothing voice that was difficult to resist. It sort of put me in a trance.

"I don't believe in God, and I don't think you can help me. All that other stuff is private."

I looked over at Kit, but she refused to make eye contact with me.

"I've got to go home. This is crazy," I said, trying not to cry. "How could you tell him all those things?"

"I'm trying to reach out to you here. Please don't be mad at Kit." He held my hand, and as soon as I felt his touch, I started to weep. He rubbed my arm while I sat down. Kit took off to get some napkins.

While tears streamed down my face, Pastor Rick told his story.

"I'm sure you know I used to deal drugs. When I was twelve, I stole cars with my older brother. I looked up to him so much. He was everything to me. By the time I was sixteen, we were committing robbery. Then I got into dealing hard drugs."

It took me a moment to digest all of this.

"I got out of jail after three years for good behaviour. I was a changed man. You know what changed me? God. God helped me turn my back on that life... My brother wasn't so lucky."

"What happened?" I asked.

"He's dead."

"I'm sorry," I said.

"I never got to help him. I know he could have loved Jesus like me. But he was killed in a knife fight over a drug deal. I swore I wouldn't end up like that. And then I was saved. I'm now nineteen—happy, clean, and loving Jesus." He looked up. "Amen."

The spell was broken, and I started getting skeptical. "You don't look nineteen."

"That's what hard living will do." He shook his head sadly.

"Your story sort of sounds like a TV movie I watched the other night. I mean, it has the same plot."

He put his hand on his chest. "Stories like mine are all too familiar. So many girls like you end up on the street. With your background, you're a target."

"No one would want to sell me as a prostitute."

Pastor Rick laughed meanly. "The more damaged the better." He looked intently at me. "I could have you hooked on coke or heroin like *that*." He snapped his fingers.

Kit stared at him, still very high, with her mouth agape.

"Come to our youth group meetings," he demanded.

"Yeah, you gotta come," Kit said.

Pastor Rick looked at Kit and put his finger over her mouth to shush her.

"I've done the church thing, Rick. I'm not into it."

"God is giving you this last chance," he said. "He sent Pastor Rick to you for a reason. You can listen to him or turn your back. The choice is yours. But if you happen to die in a bus accident on the way home today, you go to hell. No second chance. That's it. Like my brother."

His eyes formed tears. He wiped them and sniffed, a little show that, from the look of it, he had performed many times.

"You think your brother is in hell?" I asked.

"I know it."

"But what if I'm a good person?"

"Doesn't matter. Unless you accept Jesus into your heart, you won't be saved."

"God is kind of an asshole then," I said.

Kit grabbed my hand and dragged me to the bathroom.

"We make fun of people who wear acid-washed jeans," I said. "Also he's too old for you."

Kit went into a stall to pee.

"Do you believe his story about his brother? It sounds made up to me," I said.

"That's not nice. His brother died and he cries about it all the time." Kit came out of the stall and washed her hands.

"He's trying to brainwash me. Don't you feel brainwashed?" I asked.

"No, he's just worried about you, and so am I. When the world ends, you'll be left behind. And you know what?" Kit said.

"What?"

Kit teared up. "We won't be able to be best friends anymore." She hugged me tightly. "Please just hear him out. Try to have an open mind."

When we got back to the table, Pastor Rick said, "Come to one meeting. If you don't like it, don't come back."

"Let me think about it," I said.

Kit slammed her hand down in frustration. "Aren't you listening to anything he's been saying? You're going to hell, and I don't want you to."

"Every minute you don't accept Jesus as your saviour, you're risking eternal damnation. We can save you right here, right now," Pastor Rick said in a way that sounded like he was closing a sale. He squeezed my hand again. "Just say the words."

For a moment, I almost got sucked in again, and then I pulled away. "No thank you."

He stood up, looked at Kit, and took her hand. "You take care. Have a safe trip home," he said, like he was willing something terrible to happen to me so he could prove himself right.

She left with him and didn't even say goodbye. I was losing my friend and I couldn't do anything to stop it. I watched them make their way out of the food court.

Instead of taking the bus, I walked home in the winter cold

with my one wet foot freezing to the point of frostbite—all to avoid that freak bus accident that would send me to hell.

* * *

A few months later it was Tammy's birthday. Farah decided to throw Tammy a party because her parents were going out of town.

I was invited but declined the invitation. Normally I wouldn't miss such a party with no parents at the end of the school year. But I couldn't bear being around everyone from the youth group, and I wanted to avoid another run-in with Pastor Rick.

Kit begged me to go and promised me this wasn't a church party. The only people from the youth group invited were Farah and Kit. After her last stunt, I didn't believe her. I was scared this was another conversion tactic.

She promised that the party was not going to be dry. Tammy, Farah, and Kit had all planned to break their vows together.

I stole a bottle of vodka from my mother's bedroom, still not quite believing this was going to be a real party like old times. I even brought some joints in case that line could be crossed too.

At the party everyone was sitting around in a circle, drinking and smoking.

When I asked what prompted the breaking of their vows, they said they didn't know. Just as they all had been converted together, they became unconverted together, a flip of a switch.

Pastor Rick got wind of the party and called Farah's house. He wanted the address and threatened to come over, but no one would give it to him.

One by one he talked to Tammy, Farah, and Kit, who had recently broken up with him. He asked each of them what was going on and who had organized this party. Then he read them scriptures and prayed for their souls.

Each one of them covered the mouthpiece as they talked to him so he couldn't hear them laughing.

When he found out that I was there, he wanted to talk to me too. I tried to refuse, but Kit shoved the phone in my ear. "You have to take a turn," she said.

I thought I would be angry hearing his voice. He had been responsible for many sleepless nights because he scared the shit out of me that day in the mall by condemning me to hell. It took several conversations with my mother to shake the feeling that no matter what I did or believed I would be doomed. I wasn't religious, but I was superstitious. When someone tells you you're going to hell for eternity, it's hard not to believe them.

Pastor Rick took my friends away from me and made them all hate themselves and feel guilty about who they were and the things they did. He shamed them and then they shamed me.

But here on the phone with a lively party in the background, he just sounded defeated, pathetic.

I didn't gloat or get defensive when he said: "This is your doing."

"This wasn't me. I'm just a guest here."

"Tell me what's going on?" he asked.

"Tammy is opening presents. Farah is cutting the cake. Everyone is sitting around and having a good time," I said.

"What's a good time?" he asked.

"People are talking, laughing, and happy," I said.

His judgmental tone seemed to fade. He got quiet and then asked me to describe what each person was doing and I told him—although I didn't tell him when they did lines of cocaine, fearing he might call the police.

The others had lost interest in playing hot potato with

Pastor Rick. Some went outside to smoke cigarettes, others headed to the back bedroom to devour the joints Kit found in my cigarette package.

"Are they drinking?" he asked.

"Yes, they're drinking," I said.

"Are you drinking?"

"Yes, I'm drinking."

"Are you worried you'll turn out like your mother?" he asked.

I didn't answer.

The party got bigger and bigger, and for some reason, I just stayed on the phone with Pastor Rick.

He told me about his childhood and brother, and I listened to him speak without commenting. He wasn't trying to convert me, but he was trying to keep me on the line as long as he could because he knew if we got disconnected, no one would answer his call again that night. They were all lost to him.

An hour later Kit saw me and said in a tone that was more accusation than question, "Are you still talking to Pastor Rick?"

I nodded.

"What are you doing?" she laughed. She was stoned out of her fucking mind.

I shrugged. "I'm talking to Rick," I said.

"Is that Kit?" Rick said. "Let me talk to her."

I held out the phone to her.

She shook her head and mouthed, *Hang up now.*

And I did.

FUCK TRUCK

When we were in university, Thea and I used to play a game to see who could get a stranger's phone number first at the bar. She usually won. I was only mildly interested in the game because I was recovering from a recent breakup, and I never wanted to go home with any of these guys.

The game occurred every Thursday because Thursday was ladies-drink-free night, aka the only night we could afford to drink aka date rape night, we joked, but the punchline wasn't funny—which we realized the night we found ourselves in a white van with guys we had met at the bar. When we got in the van, the van stopped being a van, and the guys started calling it a "Fuck Truck." The guys stopped being the nice guys from the bar and started being men we were afraid of.

The bar was located on Crescent Street near Concordia University, where Thea and I studied English literature.

It was at this bar we helped ourselves to Singapore sling after Singapore sling. Sometimes we drank Long Island iced tea. Rarely we drank beer because we thought it made us bloated. We could drink as much as we wanted for free, and all we had to do was leave a tip. Often we got black-out drunk. Often we would be sick in the morning and have to stay in bed all day. We would have blinding headaches as we tried to remember the fuzzy details of the night before, check our purses for the numbers we claimed we got from guys we talked to.

We took creative writing classes and women's studies classes. We read *Ms.* magazine. We went to poetry readings. We got outraged about men who abuse women. We mourned the École Polytechnique massacre. We volunteered for the

Quebec Public Research Interest Group and stuffed envelopes for a fundraiser to help homeless girls. We worried about the Scarborough rapist. We saw the names of dead girls on billboards.

Dead girls hung over us like rain clouds. It seemed like every other week another one missing, another one in the news.

But we thought we could handle ourselves. We used the sleazy premise of the bar to our advantage, to be ironic. Get free drinks. Have a fun night out, for peanuts. We had rules. We never left a drink unattended. We never left the other alone. We never went to any stranger's house. We never got in anyone's car. It was safe. It was easy.

Why did we get into the Fuck Truck? We didn't know.

I was so drunk I couldn't see. "I don't even know where I live," I said out loud, and Thea kicked me so hard I could feel a bruise forming. It sobered me up instantly.

"I do," she said firmly, clearly. Thea had a look in her eye that made me realize we were in some kind of trouble, in danger. She had a look in her eye that let me know she was scared and I should shut the fuck up, which I did.

There were three guys in the van, two in the front, and Thea and I in the back with the third. They had seemed like nice guys at the bar, and after, when we all got food at a nearby diner and laughed and joked—about what I have no idea because what would we have had in common with engineering students.

After we ate and almost everyone but me had sobered up a little, they offered to drive us home. If I hadn't been so shit-faced, I would have declined. I was always the one to decline, a ride or going home with someone I didn't know. I was always the responsible one, the one who was no fun, but this night I was so drunk I couldn't see, so when they offered, I said, "Sure," and we got in.

The guys looked harmless. Were they harmless? And if they

were harmless, why were they trying to scare us by calling the van a Fuck Truck and then laughing and laughing and laughing—a joke between them about us. Maybe they were playing some kind of game too. A shadow seemed to wash over the inside of the van; where once we had been flirting and laughing and having a good time, now we were frightened.

I squeezed my hands together and told myself that if I got out of here alive, I would never do this again—as if someone trying to scare or humiliate or kill me was somehow my fault.

I asked them where they grew up in hopes that whatever they were going to do, they might reconsider if I put their own families on their mind.

I knew of course this could backfire if they had a terrible relationship with their mother, but it was worth a try.

One guy said he was from Toronto, the other Newfoundland, and the third, the guy in the back with us, said, "Why are you asking so many questions?"

It was him I was scared of most. He was the one who seemed like he didn't want to be there, and that he resented his friends talking to us all night and was looking for some kind of payback.

"We live in the opposite direction," Thea said firmly.

"We thought we'd go for a drive," the driver said.

"I can't," Thea said. "I have to work in the morning." She was good at lying, but the key thing here was to not let on that we were afraid.

I noticed Thea inching toward the door. The front-seat passenger had put on the radio and a Black Sabbath song played loudly. Thea put her fingers on the door handle and wrapped her hand tightly around it. At a stoplight, she pulled the handle down. But the door was locked.

"What are you doing?" the guy in the back with us asked.

Before anyone knew what was happening, I reached behind her and pulled the lock up. Thea opened the door, and we both fell onto the street. A car narrowly missed us, and the driver screamed in French.

"Get back in," one of the guys from the van said. "We'll drive you home. We were just kidding. We were joking around."

When we didn't answer, the guy in the back said, "Crazy bitches." A car honked behind them and they sped off, tires screeching.

Thea and I got to our feet, bloodied and scraped, and made our way to the sidewalk, where a passerby asked if we were all right.

We gasped for air and hugged tightly. I was crying. Thea was crying.

"Why did we get in that van?" I asked.

"Because they seemed nice," she said.

YELLOW STICKY NOTES

When I was in university, people didn't talk about anxiety in the way they do now. If you were like me and you had it, you mostly hid it and pretended it wasn't happening.

I would count the seconds until a class was over so my heart would stop racing and I could breathe.

It often happened in classes where the professors lectured, like my Victorian literature class or my Milton class or my American drama class or my political philosophy class. I liked these classes, but having to sit still and listen made me feel panicked.

I couldn't focus on what the professor was saying. All I could do was think about how I could leave without making a spectacle of myself.

I imagined elaborate scenarios where I passed out and an ambulance had to be called or I tripped and fell spectacularly with everyone looking at me, annoyed that I had spoiled a class they were paying good money for.

I imagined the professors ignoring me and continuing on with their lecture in the same monotone voice that made me feel trapped.

As I sat frozen in my seat while my classmates took notes or joined in the class discussions, these images played over and over in my mind until it was time to leave.

Consequently I skipped a lot of my lectures and didn't do very well in school.

Once I began taking creative writing classes, the anxiety dissipated a little because writing and talking about writing helped distract me.

The class where I really forgot about my anxiety was screenwriting.

There was only one screenwriting course in the program, which was taught by a professor who had a reputation for harassing his students. The rumours involved him losing his job at another university because of a sexual harassment allegation.

Each year, women who had taken his classes would warn the women who came after them.

They would say: "Don't be alone with him" or "Watch out for the yellow sticky notes" or "Don't take his class." He made his office hours mandatory and sometimes when a student would show up to their scheduled appointment, they would find a note telling them to go somewhere else, like a coffee shop or a bar or his apartment. He only did this with women.

Even though I was wary about taking his class, I really wanted to learn how to write screenplays, so I convinced myself it wouldn't happen to me and then conveniently put it out of my mind.

I'm not quite sure why I thought nothing would happen to me, because my experience of the world had taught me otherwise. If something bad was going to happen, likely it would happen to me.

Rather than thinking he was a creep, my first impression was that he was strict and sometimes mean to students in class. If you weren't paying attention or asked a stupid question, he would humiliate you in some way. He basked in his authority of being in charge of a classroom, like a security guard who enjoys kicking teens out of a mall.

Once, just as class was starting, he caught me reading a newspaper and told me to pay attention, like I was a child. I was mortified and never did that again. Students were expected to participate in class discussions and there were many homework assignments to take up. The stakes felt high in this class, and I was eager to please.

* * *

When I went for my first meeting with this professor, I had trouble breathing and my heart was racing—I was having a panic attack. I didn't usually visit with professors, and it made me nervous to talk to one outside of class, especially this one who could be cruel. I also was seeking approval and validation. I wanted to be good at screenwriting more than I had wanted to be good at anything else.

But despite my fears, the professor was very kind and helpful outside of class. He assisted me with my script idea and complimented my writing. I felt like I was good at something. It was disarming. All the rumours fell away, as did his intimidating personality.

I looked forward to the screenwriting class and was getting straight As and participating in class discussions for the first time in my life. My panic attacks were few and far between. I thought about screenwriting non-stop. I watched every film that was recommended in class. I read scripts. I completed all of my homework.

Around the midpoint of the term, I had my second meeting with him to discuss a comedy I was writing about a woman who was losing her mind because her apartment was infested with mice. I was to meet him at 5:00 p.m. but was running late and rushed to his office, where I found the door closed. At first, I thought he had left because I was late, but then I saw it. Attached to the office window was a yellow sticky note with my name on it, the name of a nearby Italian restaurant, and a small hand-drawn map.

At first, I was confused and then my stomach lurched. Suddenly the rumours about him came flooding back.

I didn't know what to do. If I blew off the meeting, I would get a grade penalty in the only course I was excelling at and excited about, and if I went to the meeting, I could be putting myself in a troubling situation.

I was leaning toward going and began rationalizing to myself all the reasons I should go: the last meeting I had had with him was good; he didn't seem creepy; I needed help with my script so I could get a good mark.

But in truth, I pulled the note with my name on it off the office door and walked over to the restaurant because I wanted to receive more compliments about my writing.

When I got to the restaurant, I was still holding the sticky note, which the dampness of my palm had made wet. At the very end of the restaurant, I saw the professor sitting with a blond woman. I couldn't tell who she was because the back of her head was facing me, so I stayed by the entrance, thinking that maybe he was in a meeting with another student and I should wait until they finished.

After a few moments, the host asked if he could seat me. I told him I was waiting for someone and looked over at the professor. The host said, "Oh, of course, right this way," like he was expecting me. I followed him to the table where the professor was sitting and finishing up dinner with the woman who he introduced to me as his sister. She smiled nicely but wasn't too interested in meeting me. They appeared to be having an intense conversation.

"Please sit," the professor said, pointing at the chair beside him.

A server approached and asked what I would like to order, and I said, "Just water, please." I had no money on me or a credit card, and I didn't expect the professor to pay.

After the introductions, the professor and his sister continued with their conversation. I gathered that their brother had died, his belongings were in storage, and they were making arrangements about what to do with the locker and its contents. The siblings looked nothing like one another, and I wondered if one of them had been adopted or had a different parent or maybe they were step-siblings. I had the luxury of time to mull over their relationship because they continued to talk as if I wasn't there.

It reminded me of all the times in high school when my friend Alyssa would make out with her boyfriend in front of me. The three of us would be hanging out, and then suddenly they would just make out like I wasn't in the room with them. Like I wasn't a person. Perhaps they got a kick out of it or it was some kind of kink. I would sit frozen in my seat, looking down at my hands, hoping for the moment to pass. It never seemed to pass quickly enough, and it never occurred to me to get up and leave. How bad must someone feel about themselves to stay in a situation when they are being humiliated? And here I was with the professor and his sister doing a similar thing, but instead of making out, they were talking about their dead brother and their strange family dynamics.

When his sister excused herself to go to the bathroom, I asked if perhaps I got the time wrong for our meeting.

The professor shoved the last of his pasta into his mouth and wiped his chin. "No, you didn't," he said, shaking his head. "We're just finishing up." And we sat there in silence until his sister came back.

While she was waiting for her bill to be settled up, the professor and his sister got into an argument about their other brother, who had not pitched in at all for either the funeral expenses or the cost of the storage locker.

As they were arguing and the moment was getting tenser and tenser, my panic began to resurface. I didn't want to stay and witness this fight, yet I didn't know how to excuse myself from the situation. It was awkward. Painfully awkward. And I began to hyperventilate, so I went to the bathroom.

I sat on the toilet seat with my backpack and pulled out my notebook on which I had written the three questions I had about my script: Did I have an inciting incident? Was my protagonist's goal clear? And did my dialogue sound natural? The script was due in two weeks, and I was anxious to get some feedback. I held my notebook so I could focus on the questions and not on my panic. I tried to take as long as possible in the washroom so that by the time I returned, the professor's sister would be gone.

When I came back, they were still at it. But my presence seemed to cool things down momentarily. After one final tense exchange, the professor's sister left without acknowledging me.

The restaurant was empty, and it seemed to take her a long time to get to the front door. The professor did not say anything as he watched her leave.

"Maybe we should reschedule our meeting," I suggested.

"No, no," the professor said.

It felt weird for both of us to be sitting on the same side of the table, so I offered to move across from him.

"Stay where you are," he said in his strict teacher voice, and I obeyed. Then he waved over the server and told him he would like to start a new tab. After ordering a gin and tonic for himself, he asked me what I wanted to drink.

"I'm fine with water," I said.

"No, no," said the professor. "Like a drink. Like a beer. Don't you want a beer?"

I would have loved a beer in this moment. I would have loved nothing more, but I didn't have any money on me. I couldn't order a beer and not be able to pay for it. And the professor wasn't indicating that the drink would be on him.

"No, thank you," I said. Drinking with a professor seemed really weird, and the rumours about him were floating around my mind again.

"Come on. Have a drink." He was urgent and insistent, and it felt less like an offer and more like a demand.

"I can't," I said. "I have an essay due for my English class," I lied. "I'm going to the library after this."

After the waiter left to get the professor's order, he stared down at the table like he was deep in thought.

I wondered if I should ask him about my script. Had our student-teacher meeting started? Was he upset about his sister and his dead brother?

"I'm sorry about your brother," I said.

"Oh," he laughed, nodding.

I was unsure about what was happening or what to do next, so I did nothing.

A few moments later, the waiter brought him his drink. The professor thanked him sharply. It wasn't a friendly thank-you. And the server took the hint and left the table immediately.

Then the professor got a strange look on his face and said angrily, "Meeting's over."

I said, "I just had a couple of questions about—"

"Ask me next week," he said, dismissing me with his hand. He pulled out some papers from his briefcase and began to look through them.

I put on my jacket and gathered up my backpack. My face burned and I wanted to cry. "See you in class," I said before I left, but he didn't respond.

When I got on the street, I was heavy with regret and confusion. I replayed what had happened in the restaurant and couldn't make any sense of it. Was he mad that I had witnessed a private moment between him and his sister? Was he upset with his sister and taking it out on me? Was he mad I didn't have a drink with him? I could not figure it out.

I called my boyfriend, Roan, collect from a phone booth because I didn't have twenty-five cents and told him what had happened, to which he responded: "That is fucking weird, and what an asshole."

The next class, I was worried I was somehow in the professor's bad books, but when I came in, he said hello in an unusually friendly tone and set up a new day for us to have our office hour.

I had decided before I went that if there was another note, I would not show up. If there was a sticky note, I would not follow its directions, no matter where it took me. I had no intention of going through another excruciating experience like I had that day at the restaurant.

But much to my surprise, when I did show up, he was sitting in his office like the first meeting, and he immediately began talking about my script. He asked me to outline the plot and gave me some pointers on the structure. It was normal and professional, and I left even more confused.

For the rest of the term, the professor continued to act like nothing had ever happened, and I played along.

HARD TO GET

When I was in my early twenties, I was waiting for a bus on a cold winter day around the Christmas holidays. I had been shopping for a gift for my boyfriend's family, who were throwing a small party that night. I had no idea what to get them, so I settled on a fruit basket. Roan and I had been dating less than a year, and we'd only been living together for about four months, so I didn't know his family very well, but I liked them and they seemed fun compared to mine.

A bus—not the one I was waiting for—pulled up, and two drivers who had just finished their shift got out and began to talk to each other. One of them looked over at me and said, "Hey, cutie, come on over and talk to us." He had red hair and a red beard and a loud obnoxious voice that could be heard clearly all the way down the street.

I said, "No," and he proceeded to call me a bitch and a whore. It escalated so fast I was in shock for a moment.

The other driver put his arm on his friend's shoulder and told him to stop, to smarten up.

Normally I would ignore a man who was shouting obscenities at me, for fear of a terrible outcome. Because he was still in his city bus driver uniform and we were on a busy street, something snapped in me, and I just laid into him. I yelled and swore and told him he was a pig who should be fired for being drunk on the job.

He called me a cunt and said I was ugly and to go fuck myself. I called him an asshole and told him to go fuck himself, and this back and forth of insults went on for a good long time until I said I was going to report him to the transit commission. At that, his buddy had the good sense to drag him away.

As promised, when I got home, I reported him. I told them what had happened, the time of day, his description, his friend's description, and his bus number, hoping to get him into some serious shit, if not fired.

* * *

We arrived at Roan's parents' party a little late that night. His sister and her husband were there, along with Roan's aunts, uncles, and cousins—all of whom I was meeting for the first time. I was nervous about making a good first impression.

After everyone had had a couple of drinks, someone knocked at the door.

"That's probably my dad," said the fiancée of one of Roan's uncles. "He's stopping in for a drink."

I froze when I heard a booming obnoxious voice in the front hall that I immediately recognized. A middle-aged man with red hair and a red beard walked into the living room and greeted everyone with a big smile and holiday cheer.

It was the bus driver who had harassed me on the street.

There are so many things you think you will do in a moment like this, a moment of unbelievable coincidence where there is the potential for revenge.

Of course, I wanted to point at him and tell everyone in the room that this man had harassed me today and I had reported him to his boss.

But I did not do this. In fact, I couldn't move as I watched him making his way around the room like he was a celebrity.

I hoped he wouldn't recognize me and was about to beeline for the washroom when my boyfriend's parents stopped me and introduced us.

I saw the recognition in his eyes as he grabbed my hand to shake it. I looked at him with pure hate.

He held his grip firmly on my hand as he wished me a happy holiday and tried to kiss my cheek.

I pulled my hand back abruptly and refused the kiss. "No thanks," I said loudly and in a tone I hoped he perceived as a threat.

Everyone in the room turned to look at us.

He laughed off the rejection and said to no one in particular, "She's playing hard to get."

I WON'T CLEAN THE TUB

I worked as a cleaner in a small Montreal hotel the summer I graduated from university. It was a four-storey grey building near Mount Royal. Cleaners were instructed to knock on all doors before entering and to never clean a room if a guest was still occupying it. Doors were always to be left open.

I remember being told these rules during my training, but I was focused on learning how to correctly make a bed, which I always failed to get right.

My boss was a harsh woman who looked more like a ballet teacher than a hotel operator. She wore green dresses and a strong perfume that lingered in the hotel rooms and hallways long after she had checked on my work. She was very concerned about my hospital corners.

"Why can't you learn to do this properly?" she would say as she demonstrated for me for the tenth time how to make a bed.

Working at this hotel is where I discovered the custom of leaving tips for cleaners. Once I got a twenty-dollar bill. I was afraid it was too much money, so I took it to my boss.

"What should I do with it? Should I keep it?" I asked.

"Why shouldn't you keep it?" she said. "They left it for you. Of course you should keep it."

Despite complaining about my bed-making ability and that I worked too slowly, my boss left me alone most of the time while she worked the front desk.

The best rooms to clean were on the third and fourth floors. These rooms were the brightest and biggest and had blue and green and yellow floral curtains and bedspreads. Each had a small desk for letter writing, supplied with hotel stationery and pens. The biggest room had a loveseat I liked to sit in. Often these rooms had families staying in them, their tourist pamphlets spread out on the bed or on the dresser. I would look through the pamphlets even though I wasn't supposed to.

I wanted to be these people travelling to the art galleries in Old Montreal, stopping for lunch, having café au lait on a patio. I did not want to be me, who was not only not travelling but also scrubbing pubic hair off their toilet so it would be clean for them when they returned from sightseeing.

The worst rooms to clean were in the basement. These were single-occupancy rooms where mostly older men stayed for long-term accommodations. The basement smelled musty and was dark. The windows were small, the rooms no bigger than closets. The men who stayed in them never tipped.

I got to the basement on a particularly quiet afternoon well after three. I knew I was behind schedule, but also that there was only one room to clean. I quickly grabbed the metal doorknob and knocked. There was no answer. I knocked again and said, "Maid service," but heard nothing, so I pulled out my key and opened the door. The room was dark and the curtains were shut. A man around forty was sleeping on the single bed near the door. I apologized and retreated into the hall, but he said, "It's all right. Just clean while I'm in here. I want the garbage taken out and new towels. You don't need to vacuum."

I paused for a moment. "I'm not supposed to clean while guests are in their rooms," I said.

"It's fine. I don't mind," he said.

I left the door open and brought my cleaning supplies into the bathroom with my head down.

The room smelled of urine. The toilet looked like it hadn't been flushed in days. I turned away from it almost gagging and stood in front of the mirror. I was about to clean it when I heard the door of the hotel room click shut.

Suddenly the purpose of the open-door rule dawned on me. I tensed and felt prickles of electricity in every pore. Anything could happen down here. The tiny window in the room had three panes of glass and was sealed shut. No one ever came into the basement unless it was to clean a room. If I screamed, no one would hear me.

I was too frightened to step back into the room but said from the bathroom in a shaky voice, "I'm supposed to leave the door open."

"Oh, I don't need it open. I'm just going to be sleeping," he said.

"My boss wants us to."

He didn't answer.

I couldn't move for a moment. I had to figure out what to do. If I ran out of the room, there was a chance I could unnecessarily escalate the situation. He'd said he just wanted me to tidy the bathroom. He'd said he just wanted towels. There really was no reason to be afraid, I tried to tell myself.

I wiped the mirror quickly, my hands shaking. My throat was so dry I could hardly swallow. I said to myself over and over, I won't clean the tub. I won't clean the tub. As if declaring I wouldn't clean the tub would somehow protect me in this situation.

It was when I bent down to empty the garbage that I saw them: used condoms strewn haphazardly around the bathroom floor. And in the garbage bin, a stack of *Penthouse* magazines, which were wet.

Fear has no time for disgust in moments such as these, so I quickly emptied the bin into my garbage bag and picked up the condoms with a paper towel and threw them in too. I gave the sink a wipe, grabbed the dirty towels, and stepped back into the small, stale, dark hotel room where the man was face down, snoring.

Holding my breath, I walked across the room to the door, frightened he might grab me on the way, but he didn't. I silently berated myself for being so stupid as I turned the handle on the door. In one second, it would be over, and I would never set foot in a room with a guest in it again. Never ever, ever again.

Just as I was about to make my escape with my cart down the hall to the elevator and back up to the reception desk, with its fake rubber tree plant and my boss waiting to admonish me with a scowl, the man said, as if he had never been asleep, "Did you put the fresh towels in the bathroom, love?"

I hadn't. I forgot.

"Not yet," I said, trying not to sound afraid.

"Could you, please?" he asked.

I gathered some towels for him slowly and debated whether I would go back into the room, when I heard the basement door creak open.

It was my boss. She was walking toward me. She was furious. I smelled a strong waft of her perfume as she stood before me.

"You haven't finished yet?" she said. "Why are you so slow? You are slower than any of the other girls." Peering into the room, she saw the man on his bed and frowned.

"He wanted some fresh towels," I said in a way that almost sounded like I was defending him.

"Sir, she cannot clean the room if you are in there." My boss took the towels out of my hands and put them at the end of his bed. "If you'd like your room cleaned properly, you must leave before two-thirty."

"Fuck off, you stupid cunt," he said, and turned over on his side with his back to us.

She shut his door loudly, then looked at her watch. Her hands shook slightly, and she turned to me. "It is half past three. You should be finished by three. I cannot pay you if you take longer than anyone else to do this job. Today I'll pay you until three-thirty. Tomorrow I will not. You must learn to work faster. And you must learn to follow the rules."

I started to cry.

"Why are you crying?" she said.

"I don't know," I said, wiping my eyes. But I did know. I was crying because I was relieved.

THE LUNG SPECIALIST

How do you know when someone touches your body who shouldn't be touching your body?

You know.

Even though you tell yourself it's perfectly normal.

Oh, I'm sure it's perfectly normal that the lung specialist asked me to take my shirt off but didn't give me a gown or leave the room while I changed like every other doctor I've ever had in my entire life.

It's perfectly normal that he just gave me a random breast examination and scolded me for not doing it myself.

When someone is doing something that is not normal but pretending it is normal because they are an authority figure and they tell you you're doing something wrong—that is a tactic.

Only, my twenty-five-year-old self realized it too late.

It's like robbing someone while admonishing them for not brushing their teeth or recycling properly.

When I asked about my lungs—the actual reason I was there for the visit—he said, "Your X-rays are normal."

Immediately after, I ran to the student clinic in tears to see my own doctor—who I adored, who had diagnosed me with asthma, who I told everyone was the best doctor in the whole world—to tell him what had happened and potentially report it. "Was it normal for a pulmonologist to give a breast exam when I was there to discuss my lungs?" I asked as a wave of shame moved through me.

Without missing a beat, my doctor said, "Sometimes specialists have poor bedside manners and can be insensitive. I'm sure he didn't mean anything by it. I've known him for years."

PSYCHICS

I went to a psychic when my cat ran away. I called all the psychics in the phone book. There were only three. Two would not take money for lost pets. The third set up an appointment in her home office and just told me what I wanted to hear—that my cat was still alive even though it had been three weeks and this likely was not the case. Sometimes it's kinder to let someone give up hope than to keep stringing them along.

The psychic was my last resort, but she wasn't a good psychic. My mother went to a good psychic and everything the psychic said was true, and she put it all on tape, which my mother kept in her sweater drawer. My mother wouldn't let me listen to the tape because the psychic said mean things about me—or things my mother thought I would take the wrong way, like how she was worried about me and my high school boyfriend. She should have been worried.

The psychic also told my mother that I like cheese—which is true but also a good guess. If I was a psychic, I would tell people they liked red, orange, and yellow leaves in the fall. I would tell them they liked sunsets and kittens and hammocks. You really can't go wrong with all those likes because you'd have to be a monster to not appreciate any of those things. People who visit psychics are not monsters—just desperate, hopeful, or sad. And when I say people, I mean me.

CONTEST

When I was twenty-six, I won a haiku contest for a poem I had written about an incident my dad had with his canoe on the highway.

The poem had stirred up some controversy because readers were mad that my haiku had won and another one had not. For the next four issues of the magazine, readers wrote in how the runner-up had been robbed of the prize and that my haiku was terrible.

News of the controversy spread. Some said I cheated because coincidentally my haiku depicted a scene similar to the cover of a book written by the judge. Other readers implied that had I won because I knew him, which I did not. The CBC interviewed me about the prize-winning poem and my thoughts on the controversy. The *Utne Reader* even picked up the story and ran both mine and the favoured poem in the same issue. I wasn't offended by the hate. I found it amusing that people would get so worked up about a poem.

It felt good to win something, even if it was just for three lines.

The day I went to pick up my award, I curled my hair and spent more time than usual on my makeup. I hated the way I looked. I hated getting my picture taken.

The office was small, crowded, books everywhere. Although I was worried I would be the butt of the office joke, the publisher greeted me in a friendly way. He shook my hand and congratulated me. I had my picture taken, got my trophy and seventy-five-dollar cheque, and then left.

It was a nice day, so I decided to walk the whole way home.

Before I reached the bridge, I saw someone heading toward me, smiling as if he knew me. Sometimes I have trouble recognizing people out of context, so I squinted and smiled, hoping I would recognize this person once he got closer.

I did.

It was my high school boyfriend. He hated me. He represented a life I didn't want, a life I had avoided. Sometimes I thought he would kill me.

When I had first met him, he was sort of innocent. We met at a punk bar where we drank underage. He was cute and sweet and wrote his name on my jeans. He carried a black permanent marker with him wherever he went so he could write graffiti on tables, on bathroom stalls. He played in a band with two of his friends.

The first couple of years were okay. He was sort of a loner but sweet. He didn't smoke. He didn't drink. He didn't do drugs. He was an artist and in his spare time he liked to redraw the cover art of his favourite albums. He fussed over my grandmother and helped my mom around the house, shovelling in the winter, mowing the lawn in the summer.

But once he got into drinking and drugs, which I had introduced to him, something changed. He became possessive and paranoid. He didn't like my friends and didn't want me hanging out with them. He was jealous and angry. He read my diary and always thought I was cheating on him. Because I didn't go along with his requests, we fought all the time. Big violent fights. Once he kicked in the bathroom door of my mother's house because I locked myself in trying to get away from him.

I knew I had to get out, so I applied to university and didn't invite him to come with me. He was furious, and our last year together was the most volatile and scary.

I hadn't seen or spoken to him since we broke up. I heard

he was working in Vancouver, and when I moved there for school, I was always worried we might run into each other. After three years of being there, I forgot about him. I also found out through a friend that whole last year of high school he'd been cheating on me with a girl in our grade. Everyone knew but me. I had always wanted to confront him about this betrayal since he was so intent on believing I was the one who cheated on *him*.

And here he was approaching me with a big smile. I was stunned and blurted, "Oh my god."

We exchanged pleasantries about our families. My mom had stopped drinking and was in AA. He updated me on his siblings and parents. I told him my grandfather had died and that I was married.

"Married," he said, and grabbed my hand a little roughly, looking down at the ring on my finger. He stared at it.

"I got married last year in Las Vegas," I said.

He dropped my hand. "You're married."

I didn't say anything.

"What are you doing right now?" he said. "Let's catch up."

I should have made an excuse, but I just said, "Okay," and followed him into a nearby restaurant.

I ordered a coffee, and he ordered a beer. He paid. I let him. Then we sat down.

The place was crowded. The tables close together. I felt my heart racing. I realized that agreeing to sit with him wasn't because I was trying to be polite. It was my chance to confront him about the girl who he fucked our last year together. I was being petty, and I knew it.

I put my trophy on the table. He picked it up and asked, "What's this?"

"I won a poetry contest," I said.

"What's your poem?" he asked.

"A haiku."

He nodded, mildly interested. "Congratulations," he said.

I didn't bother to tell him that just about everyone except the judge hated the poem.

He drank his beer in one sip, then went to the counter and ordered another one. It was a self-serve restaurant.

"You sure you don't want one?" he sort of yelled across the restaurant.

I shook my head.

This was the person who I thought would kill me. The person who I woke up from nightmares thinking he would break into my house. And here I was sitting across from him chatting as if we were old friends. I was dizzy.

When he came back, he asked what I did and I told him I was studying creative writing.

"I fucking hate students," he said.

School had been the thing we fought about most. It had been what broke us up, or so he thought, but I just didn't want to be with him anymore.

I set him off by mentioning school, and he went on a rant about what he thought of art students, all students. The beer was hitting him, and he started talking louder and louder.

I knew I had to get out of there, but I couldn't let that one thing go that had bothered me for years.

"I found out that for our entire last year of high school you were fucking Samantha."

He picked at the label on his bottle. He wouldn't make eye contact with me.

"I was a different person back then," he said, clearly caught off guard.

"You used to accuse me of cheating on you. But it was you who was cheating on me." I couldn't believe I was saying these things out loud. I thought I would feel better once I said it, once I got it out of my system. But I didn't. I felt sort of sick and hollow inside.

He couldn't look at me and didn't know what to say, so he changed the subject and started telling me about his job and his boss, who he hated.

I could hardly concentrate on what he was saying because I was trying to think of how I could get out of this conversation until I blurted: "Oh no, I think I left my cat outside. I have to leave right now. He's an outdoor cat but we never leave him out unless we're home. Once he was hit by a car and it was very expensive." I rambled on and on. It was obviously a lie, and he knew it.

When I stood up, he stood up too and pulled me in for a hug that was too long and too tight.

In my rush to leave the restaurant, I forgot my trophy on the table.

WIPEOUT

I'm on the second floor of the Market, staring out the window at the skaters on the ice rink below.

There's a tiny girl, about five, who cannot stand on the ice for more than a few seconds before her arms flail and she wipes out.

Occasionally her siblings help her up but mostly she picks herself up and off she goes again, a few steps and then another spectacular fall.

She does not stop or cling to the side of the rink or cry.

This girl has no fear. She just gets back out there as if the fall had never taken place.

When I first saw her, I felt sorry for her. It was so painful to watch, I cringed and almost had to look away—but forty-five minutes later, watching her fall over and over and over, determined as ever to get back on the ice, I realize that she's going to be okay.

This Isn't a Conversation

—Let's say you live on a planet with limited resources and a complex biosphere, and all your activities threaten the survival of all species including your own. What do you do?

—Let's pretend happiness.

—What if scientists discover that Canada is warming two times faster than the rest of world and no one does anything about it?

—I think I've seen that movie before.

—How does it end?

—Not well.

—Someone will take care of it.

—No one's taking care of it.

—I know you're proud of yourself, but
we happen to be facing extinction.

—It's not that bad.

—It's dire.

—Don't poison today with tomorrow.

—Worse things to come.

—There's a dark cloud overhead.

—It's you.

—You're letting the world come to an end.

—I know, right?

—Why isn't everybody screaming from the rooftops?

—Liability.

—Don't be a fatalist, dude.

—Who am I? I am nothing.

—I like being here.

—I'm imagining something better.

—Everything's a selfie, but I'm interested in your inner life.

—Do what you want but don't tell me about it.

—Tell everyone what they want to hear.

—Good luck, people.

—I've been operating in the wrong
sphere.

—Nobody cares.

—Nobody knows what to do.

—If you are going to state the obvious, please don't let it be in the form of a conversation about the weather.

—I don't think we're on the same wavelength.

—I don't think there are wavelengths.

—Can I tell you the truth? I haven't been listening to a word you've said. I've been watching your mouth move and telling myself exactly what I want to hear.

—I'm turning my rage into butterflies.

—That's convenient.

—You're being hard on me.

—Be a better person.

—I like to be on the no expectations side of expectations.

—Did we do everything we could?

—Nope.

—Sea creatures are boiling to death in their shells—in the sea.

—Yes, but how is this relevant to me?

—It's going to be hard to fulfill all your hopes and dreams during total societal collapse.

—Let's worry about something else.

—I'm practising disembodiment.

—I'm into denialism.

—Every day is the same day.

—I know, it's capitalism.

—What are your retirement plans?

—Extinction.

—I'm here for intensity.

—I'm here for magnitude.

—I don't know who needs to hear this,
but I'm sinking.

—Don't sink.

—I don't even remember what I was crying about.

—You got a story out of it.

—Wasn't worth it.

—Nothing matters. That's my fallback.

—I want to be glitzy.

—I'm in the mood for staring into the void.

—Everything becomes beautiful when you realize nothing is going to last.

—The sky is falling.

—I don't believe the sky is falling.

—Each day, a new horror.

—We're all blips.

—It seems impossible to find anything in this world that doesn't have a downside.

—You look better than I do.

—I hope environmental catastrophe doesn't interfere with your self-actualization.

—Look what I made!

—You're either interested in breathing
or you're not interested in breathing.

—One like.

—I've decided that the less I know, the happier I'll be. And if I'm happier, then I won't have to worry about what the politicians are really doing or how we are slowly killing ourselves in a murder-suicide of epic proportions.

—Insert a joke.

—I like your projection.

—What if you saw a story that said, I'm sorry I wrote this story?

—I'd say, Please save some misery for me.

—I'm going to come across as mean.
This is one of my survival skills.

—I'm trying not to be terrifying.

—When do we get to the good part?

—Don't look. It's worse than you think.

—Hey, whatcha up to?

—Just participating in the world's mass-murder-suicide event.

—How'd you get involved in that?

—By doing absolutely nothing.

—How's it going?

—Pretty fucking well.

—It's raining. I'm near it but not getting wet. Yet.

—When they said it was beautiful, I should have looked.

—I like your cloud.

—Why did you wait until today to tell me?

—I did my best.

—Nope.

—I believe in art despite not believing in art.

—Is that hope?

—Post-hope.

—It's not too late, is it?

—Depends who you ask.

—Wave to the shore before we sink.

—I'm scared.

—What scares you the most?

—My thoughts.

My Dream House

MY DREAM HOUSE

The Future had bought some land and was building their dream house with their own two hands. Even though the work was difficult and back-breaking, they felt they were up for the challenge because they were considered handy.

The Past was standing behind The Future, in yellow overalls and a backwards baseball hat, watching everything The Future was trying to do. Every once in a while, The Past would cover their mouth in an attempt to control an eruption of giggles.

After looking back at The Past with a little glare, The Future laid down some boards and hammered some nails, trying to ignore the rude and inconsiderate disruption.

But the more The Future hammered, the more The Past giggled into their palm. Eventually the giggling turned into an outright laugh and then a high-pitched cackle followed by a stream of tears.

The Future threw down the hammer and stomped over to The Past: —What is your problem? Why are you laughing like that?

The Past wiped their face and took in some gulps of badly need air. —I'm laughing, they stammered as another fit of giggles started to bubble to the surface, —I'm laughing because when I'm finished with you, there's not going to be anything left of this place.

THE BED

The Past and The Future had been sleeping in the same bed ever since they could remember.

Sometimes when The Past had a bad dream or felt scared, The Future would rub their back until they fell asleep.

Normally, however, The Past was the type of sleeper who was out cold the minute their head hit the pillow. The Past could sleep through any kind of disturbance and nothing would rouse them until the morning.

The Future, on the other hand, had a sleep disorder for which they often sought help but the doctors could never treat. Not only did they have a hard time falling asleep, but they would also wake throughout the night to pee. In the morning, The Future would have dark circles under their eyes, and it seemed as though each night they got less sleep than the night before.

The Past suggested that The Future's problem might have something to do with their bed, which was old and lumpy and uncomfortable. So they went bed shopping and found a mattress they could both agree on.

The Future worried about getting The Past's hopes up, and truth be told they didn't think a new mattress would help, but they wanted to appear as though they were doing all they could to improve the situation.

As usual, The Past crashed the minute they crawled into bed and started snoring loudly, which always irritated The Future because it made The Future feel like The Past was showing off or rubbing it in.

For a long time, The Future, whose eyes were stinging because they could not sleep, stared down at The Past, who slept noisily but with a very peaceful smile on their face. That must feel good to sleep so soundly, The Future thought.

It dawned on The Future that maybe it wasn't the bed that was causing a troubled sleep. Maybe it was The Past who was to blame for all their distress. Without a second thought, The Future covered The Past's face with a pillow and held it there for a long time.

And when The Past awoke and tried to wriggle out of The Future's grasp, The Future held on with a firm grip. They held on until their arms burned with the strain. They held on as if The Future's own life depended on it.

A LAUGH

The Past and The Future were sharing a laugh about something funny.

The Past held a stone in their right hand, and when they both averted their eyes, The Past grabbed The Future's hand and gave it a little squeeze.

Taking this as a sign, The Future leaned in for a hug.

The Past put their lips on The Future's forehead and said, —Don't kiss me.

—I wasn't planning on it, The Future said.

And they just stood there—unable to stay, unable to let go.

HOW CAN YOU GO ON?

—If I die, will you die? The Future asked out of the blue one day when it occurred to them that there might be an end to all this.

—Yes, said The Past. The Past was calm and rested their hands in their lap.

—Will we meet again in the spirit world? asked The Future.

—When we both die, there will be no worlds of any kind, said The Past.

—How can you go on knowing that one day neither of us will exist? The Future asked with tears in their eyes. —Doesn't that make you sad?

—I try deep-breathing exercises, said The Past, —and I write in my gratitude journal. Sometimes I take long walks along the beach and make up stories in my head about conversations I've never had with people I've met in passing. Sometimes the conversations lead to debates about abortion and climate change and the ever-growing class divide. Other times these conversations lead to flattery where I'm flattering the acquaintance or they are flattering me. If I'm feeling particularly low, I will photograph myself from a really good angle and post it on the internet in hopes that it will get many likes and will make others feel bad about themselves because they're them and not me. I'm lucky, I tell myself. Sometimes I believe it.

DATE NIGHT

The Past and The Future realized they were slowly growing apart and they needed to work on their relationship.

Part of the problem was that The Past didn't have any hobbies or any friends of their own. The Past was too reliant on The Future to plan their social calendar.

Because The Future was so outgoing, it made The Past want to retreat into their shell.

—This may be a deal breaker, said The Future. —I can't live with a personality like that.

Date night didn't go very well. Neither of them liked the restaurant and the people beside them were talking far too loud about world issues and their opinions, which The Future thought were ill-informed.

Every once in a while, The Future would try to talk over them, but The Past said to hush because The Future was causing a scene and really wasn't it better to not talk about these things in public and to keep all your opinions to yourself.

People from other tables were looking at The Past and The Future to see what was going on and if a fight would ensue.

For the rest of the night The Future gave The Past the silent treatment and would only communicate using their eyes and occasionally a twitch of their upper lip.

Later that night The Past read a self-help book that said it would be easier for The Past to accept themselves the way they were rather than trying to do anything to change.

Even if the cost was high. Even if it meant the end of their relationship with The Future.

I SHIT HERE

The Past and The Future were in bathing suits, taking turns running through the sprinkler when The Future saw something shiny out of the corner of their eye and ran to the far end of the yard.

It was an aluminum garbage can lid near the pink rose bushes under which thistles grew.

The Future lifted the lid.

The grass where the lid had lain was stained the colour of straw, and in the middle, a perfectly formed piece of shit—the size of a candy bar, the colour of yams.

—I shit here, The Past said.

—Why? asked The Future, a little insulted, a little confused.

—Because I like you, The Past said. —I like you a lot.

—What does that mean? asked The Future.

—It means we're entering into a dynamic that will likely be good for me and not for you and you'll go along with it because you'll feel you don't have any choice, said The Past. —But the funny thing is that you're a free agent and can do as you please, but I'm going to take advantage of the fact that you don't have a fucking clue.

Then The Past returned the lid to its original position on the grass, like they were pushing away a dinner plate.

The Future was crestfallen, so The Past gave The Future a little punch on the arm.

—Buck up, it's only for eternity, said The Past.

LIMA BEANS

The Past was trying to get The Future to eat lima beans, but they refused.

When The Past wasn't looking, The Future dropped the beans one by one in the crack between the kitchen cupboard and the wall.

No one would know.

No one would find out.

THE HOUSE FIRE

The Past and The Future were standing on the lawn awaiting the fire truck as they watched their house going up in flames.

The Future had remembered to bring a hanky on the way out and was crying into it and blowing their nose.

Actually they were weeping.

The Past was dry-eyed and yawning and complaining about it being time for bed.

The Future turned to The Past angrily: —Why aren't you upset about this? How can you even think about going to sleep?

The Past yawned again and scratched their itchy eyes. Something in the air was giving them an allergy. —It doesn't really affect me, The Past said. —I wasn't going to live here. You were.

THE VIADUCT

The Past and The Future were standing on the outer edge of the Viaduct near the distress telephone line sign.

They were looking down at the foliage and the street below. Everything looked both close and far away. It was the kind of day that was not too warm and not too cold, although there was a slight breeze that tousled their hair.

—Did you know over five hundred people have jumped from this bridge? The Past asked.

—No, I didn't know that, The Future said.

—I wonder what makes people jump? The Past asked.

—Lots of things, The Future said. —Life is a nightmare.

—Do you really think life is a nightmare? The Past asked.

—Yes, the sooner it's over the better. The Future teared up a little thinking about all the things they would miss but looked away quickly so The Past couldn't see all this emotion.

—I feel like I'm in a movie, The Future said, and leaned over the edge.

—What kind of a movie?

—A comedy, said The Future, —that is so funny it makes you weep.

—Most comedy is rooted in deep pain, said The Past, putting an arm around The Future.

—Don't touch me, The Future said.

The Past stepped away from The Future, then looked down at all the little cars below. —What are you waiting for? asked The Past.

The Future looked at the deep drop below, then turned to The Past and said: —I'm waiting for you.

THE ATTIC

The Past and The Future were cleaning out the attic, which was filled with old boxes of junk they intended to sell at the community yard sale.

The stairs to the attic were small and rickety. It was easy to trip or lose one's balance. One step had a crack, another step had a nail sticking out, and a third step was missing altogether.

Each time The Future walked up or down the stairs, they walked backwards—even if they were carrying cleaning supplies, even if they were carrying a heavy box or two.

It made for a slow and unsteady trip and was beginning to annoy The Past, who had organized a table tennis tournament for later in the day and wanted to finish and get washed up.

—Why don't you face forward when you are going up and down these stairs? The Past asked. —It's dangerous. You could fall and hurt yourself, and on your way down you could hurt me too.

—I walk backwards, said The Future, so I can keep my eyes on you.

—What do you think I'm going to do?

—Chase me up the stairs or grab my ass, said The Future.

—You think I'm the type who would do that? The Past said, utterly offended. —That really hurts my feelings.

The Future sighed and said, —Fine, I'll turn around. But if you do anything you're not supposed to, it'll be disastrous for us both.

—Trust me, said The Past. —I can't believe you won't trust me.

As soon as The Future turned their back, The Past let out

a truly sinister laugh and started chasing The Future up the stairs. As The Past took a swipe at The Future's ass, The Future tripped and they both went tumbling down the stairs, landing in a tangled heap of broken bones.

The Future laughed because there was absolutely nothing else they could do. Neither had a cellphone on them and no one knew where they were. —I guess they'll find us when our bodies rot, said The Future.

—The problem with you, said The Past, —is not just that you're right but that you enjoy being right.

THE PRESENT

The Present stood before The Future and The Past and shook their head like a disappointed parent.

—How long are you going to put up with each other's shit? You know life is short.

The Past and The Future looked at The Present very confused. —You mean we have a choice?

DO I HAVE TO BE ME?

—Do I have to be me? asked The Future.

—Yes, I'm me and you're you, said The Past.

—But I don't want to be me.

—Who do you want to be?

—I'd like to be you, said The Future.

—I'm The Past and you're The Future.

—What if I became you and you became me?

—I like being me, The Past said. It's comfortable. I don't have to think or do anything. I don't have worry about what's going to happen or try to change anything. I can decide to take a long bath or go for a nice walk. It's really nice being me. It's like sleeping on a soft bed or squeezing a favourite pillow in the middle of the night, knowing in the morning I'm certain to wake up to a warm breakfast.

—I'd like that for myself, said The Future.

—Well, maybe you can be me once I retire.

—When do you plan to retire?

—Never, said The Past.

REMOTE CONTROL

There was snow. There was ice on the sidewalk. The Future kept slipping in their runners. The Past called them runners, but they were really called running shoes—although truth be told, The Future never did much running. Some people call them sneakers. But The Future never did much sneaking either.

What did The Future do? Raced remote-controlled dune buggies whenever they got the chance. In between taking The Past to doctor appointments. In between shifts at the laundry. On hot days. On cold days. Christmas morning. The Future didn't smoke, didn't drink, just liked dune buggies.

The Past wouldn't let The Future practise in the house. The Past didn't like the noise, didn't even like the noise in the yard, so they sent The Future to the park.

But the park was a problem because of all the dogs that chased him. Him as in The Future's dune buggy named Martin. The dogs would chase Martin as if he was a toy. They would bark and slobber and bite.

And then the gas station nearby closed, and they got rid of the pumps and the building and put a wire fence around the lot. A dream come true. A dream come true. The Future's own space to practise with no distractions, with no kids asking if they could try Martin out. No dogs. Maybe the odd old nosey bugger, but The Future could put up with that.

The Past told The Future to put on winter boots when they saw the runners.

—I'm all grown-up. Don't tell me what to do.

And then The Future pushed The Past a little. Not too hard.

It was just a little push, but The Past stumbled back and tripped on the stairs.

Sometimes The Past didn't get dressed and that depressed The Future.

Sometimes The Past smelled bad because they didn't shower often enough. Sometimes The Future wished The Past wasn't alive to give them such a hard time.

The Past hit the floor before The Future could grab them. The Past hit the floor with a loud thud. Something fell off the table. Maybe a dish of peppermints or a candle.

In the commotion, The Future accidentally hit the transmitter, and Martin swerved and turned and hit The Past's veiny leg and then the coat closet. The only sound was the motor vibrating against the solid wooden door.

The Past was right. The Future's shoes didn't have enough treads, and The Future was slipping and sliding all the way to the vacant lot. It was hard to steer Martin when The Future felt so off-balance. So The Future walked a little slower over the ice but was worried about Martin and feared he might get hit by a car, so The Future steered him close.

The Future just had to open the fence a little and eased old Martin through, his motor buzzing softly in the cold winter air. And then The Future let him rip. And he was flying through the snow like a bird.

Each time he lunged through the air, The Future's heart lunged too. And their body felt like a body feels when it's in love.

BEDROOM COMMUNITY

The Past used to be tied to a table in the middle of the strip mall. But The Past's attendants had to keep cleaning The Past's clothes because so many of the residents of the adjacent suburb took to throwing tomatoes, which stained The Past's finely pressed white shirts.

After much public debate, the residents encased The Past in a glass cage in which The Past was able to roam free, untethered by ropes. And the suburb never had to fear The Past would escape because the glass was unbreakable and bulletproof—although no one, not even The Past, had bothered to test it.

Once in the glass cage, they stripped The Past of all clothes because the cage was sure to protect The Past from the elements and no one looked upon The Past as a sexual being. In the eyes of the residents, The Past was no better than a snake or a fox but not as beautiful and existing with much less purpose.

When The Past had to defecate, a black curtain was drawn, but besides that necessity, all the other activities The Past engaged in were free for public viewing. From a young age, the little children of the suburb were told to despise The Past.

The attendants were much more content now that they didn't have to do all that laundry. They enjoyed their job and didn't dread coming to work anymore. From time to time, they even got into a philosophical debate with The Past about energy and the universe and the state of manufacturing.

The Past contributed to this fate—by sheer laziness and self-importance, by fighting at meetings and not attempting to make the workplace anything other than an extension of The Past's self-interest, and, worst of all, by ignoring the structures that enabled The Past's comfort at the expense of others. It seemed as though The Past got exactly what The Past deserved. Few would disagree.

Given how the residents of this small suburb felt about The Past, you can imagine the trouble that struck them on the day The Past broke through the glass cage and ran naked into the undeveloped land near the mall also known as the forest. There was a crack in the glass that The Past noticed one day after eating a cheese sandwich for lunch. The Past waited until everyone went to bed before giving the glass a little tap, and much to The Past's delight, the whole cage shattered. Not a shard cut The Past's delicate skin. This was a sign of good things to come.

When the residents discovered The Past had escaped, alarms were sounded, and a mass email was sent to all those who had bothered to sign up. Local news and radio outlets warned residents to be careful moving around the suburb. There was a danger in the community as grave as an infectious airborne disease.

It was worse, everyone agreed, than if a serial killer were in their midst. Parents kept their children close by and locked their windows and doors. The community was told to not to go near The Past, and if one of them should come across the despised fugitive, they were instructed to call the authorities. *The Past may be dangerous,* the email said. *The Past may cause you harm. Think of The Past as you would a grenade.*

In schoolyards, pupils made up hand-clapping games about The Past that ended in fist fights and children of all ages being sent to the principal's office with bruises and bloody noses.

Groups of armed neighbours searched the woods and suburbs and garages and underground parking lots, but they found nothing other than a dead squirrel or a mauled cat. Some were genuinely worried about the effect The Past would have on their suburb, but others were more interested in the reward offered by the authorities. It was a large amount of money, a mouth-watering amount of money. It was enough to make most of the residents get off the couch and join in the search, bringing the community closer together.

For days, The Past seemed gone without a trace. Rumoured sightings amounted to nothing, and even a few copycats wound up on the streets in a pathetic cry for attention.

—Put some clothes on, an officer said to one copycat. —And go home to your parents who are worried you've become a pervert.

—When The Past is caught, The Past must be killed, the residents chanted as they charged through the woods.

They were no longer interested in tomatoes—they were after blood and money. The reward would be given whether The Past was found dead or alive.

—Oh, don't worry, my darling, they will catch The Past and they will make sure The Past never escapes again, a woman told her teenage daughter who was walking beside her with tears in her eyes. But what the woman didn't know was that she and her daughter had bigger problems than The Past, for her daughter was pregnant and had an STI.

—Maybe The Past is scared and doesn't mean us any harm, a little boy said to his father.

—Oh, no, said his father, —don't let anyone hear you say that.

* * *

It had been so long since The Past had eaten fresh fruit off the trees or felt the cool breeze. The Past waded in the stream and drank from it and remembered being a child and receiving the love of a mother and father. There were many around the supper table in The Past's youth, and The Past remembered a grandfather who smelled of tobacco and who slapped the ass of the waitress when she walked by. The Past's family had owned a farm and The Past used to marvel at life and all its wonders.

To recall these memories caused The Past's eyes to fill with tears of joy, but the joy also caused The Past some degree of pain. I guess it is in our suffering that we are most grateful, The Past thought, and touched all the green plants and smelled the beautiful flowers and imagined this was how time would be spent from now on until the final day. Then The Past came upon a pointed stone that was as sharp as a knife.

While The Past was taking in the natural world as a poet would, they failed to hear the residents hunting them down like a wild animal. The dogs had been called in and had tracked The Past's scent. They were closing in.

In the nick of time, The Past heard a rustling and hid behind a bush, shaking with fear as the residents passed by, holding their flashlights and smoke bombs.

The Future falling behind the mob saw The Past, but before they could call out, The Past grabbed The Future and stabbed them to death with the pointed stone. The Past donned The Future's clothes and purse and proceeded to follow the crowd, some of whom were starting to become uninterested in the chase.

—When we find The Past, we will kill The Past, said a woman weakly and without conviction.

They were starting to lose faith and had become unfocused and bored.

—Yes, said The Past to a man walking beside them. —We will kill The Past. No matter what.

—Do you have a mint? the man asked. —My throat is getting dry, and I wish I were at home in my bed.

As The Past felt around The Future's purse, they thought about all those tomatoes and the image made The Past's stomach lurch. —I will never eat a tomato or a cheese sandwich again, The Past vowed.

Finally, The Past produced a green mint in a plastic wrapper and presented it to the man like a trophy.

THE BUS STOP

The Past and The Future sat at a bus stop and waited for a bus that didn't come.

—It will come soon, said The Past, and lit a cigarette. —If you light a cigarette the bus will come before you have a chance to smoke it.

The Future sighed and sat down.

The sun rose and the sun set.

—I'm tired of waiting, said The Future.

—It will come, said The Past. —It's always come before. Just wait a few more minutes.

The Past finished their cigarette and lit another one, so firm was their belief that this was the order of things—light cigarette and bus will come.

—But I'm tired and hungry and my favourite TV show is on, complained The Future.

They waited and waited and waited. And still the bus still didn't come. And the cigarettes continued to burn, one after the other.

It rained and stormed and snowed and then spring came and then a heat wave.

Wildfires roared all round them. And the bus did not come.

They curled up beside each other. The Past stroked The Future's hair.

—I'm scared, said The Future.

—Me too, said The Past.

—What are we going to do? asked The Future.

—Let's get into a fight about beauty, said The Past. And then you can tell me that I don't exist, and I'll tell you that you don't exist, and we'll forget about our predicament.

—I'd rather walk home, said The Future. They held out their hand to The Past, who took it, and they walked the long way home where they could see all the flowers that had bloomed.

THE ORDER

The Past and The Future were having dinner at their favourite restaurant.

Although it was pricey, they loved everything about this place, from the service to the decor to the absolutely delicious menu. It was the kind of place that caters to your every allergy or whim.

—But you sure pay for it, The Past loved to tell anyone who listened. The Past liked to brag that they'd made a comfortable life for themselves and to insist that it was okay because they deserved it.

This is the restaurant where The Past and The Future celebrated birthdays and anniversaries and special dates with friends. It really was their home away from home.

As the waiter rolled a cart toward their table, The Past stuck out their tongue greedily.

—I'm absolutely famished, The Future said. —I cannot wait to eat.

The server set down the plates and lifted the lids with a dramatic gesture. Steam rose from the hot dishes.

They ate, eagerly taking big gulps of water between bites.

But after a few moments, The Future realized something was terribly wrong and spat out a mouthful of food into their napkin. —This isn't what I ordered, The Future said to The Past.

—You should send it back, said The Past. —You shouldn't have to eat something you didn't order.

The Past tried to get the server's attention. —Excuse me, The Past said, but to no avail.

—Oh, forget it. I'll make do, The Future said, looking down at the meal in disgust

—That's ridiculous, said The Past. —He's right there. Get his attention.

—Excuse me, said The Future, who was not normally the type to send their meal back to the kitchen, or at least that's what they told themselves about their own personality. —I hate to complain, but I ordered Life on Earth, and you brought me Extinction.

—The kitchen is all out of Life on Earth, the server explained.

—This used to be such a good restaurant, the Past said, even though their meal was perfectly fine and they devoured it.

—Am I expected to pay for what I didn't order? The Future asked.

—Yes, said the server pointing to the menu. —It's in the fine print.

TUG-OF-WAR

The Past and The Future stood in the middle of the schoolyard. A crowd of onlookers were huddled toward the back, where the branches from a neighbouring tree provided some much-needed shade.

It was a blistering hot day.

On the ground between them lay a thick braided rope.

The Past and The Future each picked up an end and pulled it taut.

The Present, who was acting as a referee for the game, held the rope in the middle, then looked at everyone like an annoyed grade-school teacher.

The crowd shushed one another and settled in.

Then The Present stepped back and said to The Past and The Future: —You may begin.

The Past pulled the rope hard, taking The Future, who momentarily lost their footing, by surprise. Then The Future gripped the rope tighter and yanked it so that The Past fell to their knees and skinned them. Without missing a beat, The Past got back up as blood oozed from the fresh wound and dripped onto the ground.

As they each kept their grip on the rope, their brows filled with sweat.

The hemp burned their hands. One cried out and then the other cried out. Their pain seemed to make the crowd cheer.

Neither was in particularly good shape. Neither had been going to the gym. But The Past had once been athletic in their youth, which gave them the upper hand despite the knee injury.

The Past came back hard at The Future, but The Future

regrouped and dominated. Everyone agreed that it was an even match.

Still, the onlookers were fickle.

When it looked as though The Past was winning, they cheered for The Past. When it looked as though The Future was gaining the upper hand, they cheered for The Future.

And The Present? Well, The Present was furiously taking notes throughout the match, looking up once in a while, then madly scribbling.

But The Present wasn't watching the tug-of-war at all—they were composing a love poem to someone they admired from afar who had no idea they were the object of The Present's affection.

The Present thought about this person all the time. It was keeping The Present up into the wee hours of the morning. The Present couldn't eat and couldn't sleep. And it was having an impact on The Present at work and with friends and family. Oh, but the love poem was so beautiful and so heartfelt. It had words in it like *shimmer* and *undulation*. Too bad no one would ever get to read it because The Present tore it to pieces when the object of their love found someone else.

As for the game? Well, The Past and The Future continued their tug-of-war for eternity—no one winning, no one losing.

CHILDREN

The Future and The Past were having a play date with their children in The Future's new swimming pool.

When The Future went inside to get some snacks, The Future's child began swimming in the deep end while The Past's child got out and sat in the burning sun.

—Are you having a good time? The Past asked.

Their child nodded and said, —Yes, but that kid can't swim.

The Past looked at the deep end and saw The Future's child had drowned.

Instead of rushing over to help, The Past went back to enjoying their fruity drink and menthol cigarette, accidentally ashing the top of their own child's head.

The Future finally emerged with peanuts and chips and saw their dead child floating face down in the water. —What happened? The Future asked.

—Your child drowned, The Past said.

The Future burst into tears. —I should have known better than to leave them with you. You just care about your own children.

—That's not true, The Past said. —I don't care about them either.

THE SUNBURN

On a particularly hot day in July, The Past was sunbathing on the wooden deck when The Future barked: —That's not good for you.

The Past didn't reply because they were in that half-awake, half-asleep state they so often enjoyed.

The Future shook their head at The Past and got into a little white motorboat to go fishing for pike. The Future had a bucket of minnows, a net, a rod, a fish bat, and even a little cooler for some beer and a snack. The sky was blue and the water was still. It truly was the most perfect day to fish.

The Future didn't say when they'd be back and The Past had not bothered to ask.

Neither The Past nor The Future had decided what they were going to make for dinner. The Past had a vague memory of some frozen hamburger defrosting on the kitchen counter but couldn't remember if had been set out yesterday morning or today. In either case, the hamburger would likely be spoiled.

The sun was setting on the lake and the whole sky turned a beautiful orange and red and grey. When The Past finally woke up, they were burnt, and blisters had formed all over their shoulders, stomach, arms, and legs.

Every movement caused The Past to wince and cry out at the searing pain. It was so bad even tears formed.

Realizing it was getting late, The Past took off their sunglasses and scanned the lake for a sign of The Future.

But there was none.

Not a single boat could be seen along the horizon.

—That's strange, The Past said, a little puzzled, a little shocked. —I just assumed The Future would always be there.

AT THE BAR

The Past and The Future sat on stools in a local pub, and The Past took a generous sip of their stout.

—I wish we could still smoke in bars. I'm dying for a cigarette, said The Past.

The Future was drinking Scotch and had their eye on the hockey game playing on a TV across the bar.

—I used to be so great. I used to be worthwhile, said The Past.

The Future shook their head: —Actually, you never were that great.

—That's not true. I did plenty of good things. Everyone liked me. Everyone wrote my name on their pencil cases, said The Past.

—You looked good on paper. But doing terrible things and covering it up isn't the same as always being good, said The Future.

—Is it my fault that nobody noticed my faults until now? asked The Past. The Past put their head down and started to cry. Puddles of tears formed on the bar top.

The bartender came by and wiped up The Past's tears.

—Stop that. You're staining the wood, said the bartender.

—I used to be somebody. And now I'm a wash-up with hives and eczema, said The Past.

—The problem with you is that you bought into the myth about yourself, said the bartender, —and this has proven to be a very dangerous thing.

—But so did everyone else! said The Past.

—Now they don't, said The Future with a little laugh.

YOU DON'T EXIST

The Past, The Future, and The Present were enjoying the hot tub on a cool evening.

The Past's back was sore and The Future was practising mindfulness.

The Present looked at them both and frowned. —I feel left out when I'm around you two.

—Here we go, said The Past.

The Future made a soft humming sound to block out the chatter because they had just reached the point where they could divert every thought as it came into their mind.

—Seriously, said The Present, you two are a clique.

—Have you ever considered, said The Past, —that you may feel left out because you might not even exist? In fact, you—or rather the concept of you—may be an impossibility.

The Present shook their head and started to laugh. — Hilarious. That's just so funny I could weep. My therapist says it's okay to let go of people who are having a negative impact on your life. I think he has a point. I have some theories about you, but I wouldn't be so rude as to say them to your face. I was telling you how I felt when I'm with you two. I was expressing myself in order to deepen our relationship. You don't need to tell everyone everything you think about them if it's going to hurt their feelings.

—Sorry, but I have an honesty problem, said The Past. — And when I lie, people see right through me.

—Would you two knock it off? said The Future. —I'm trying to meditate and move into a deep state of relaxation.

The Present shook their head and lifted themselves out of the hot tub.

The Past watched The Present grab a towel and head toward the house.

—Are you naked? The Past asked.

—I'm wearing swim trunks, said The Future, who looked over at The Present's bare ass shining in the moonlight.

—I am too, said The Past, and they laughed together about The Present's nakedness.

—We're awful, howled The Past.

—It's true. It's true, cried The Future, who laughed so hard they got a stitch in their side.

TUMBLE IN THE HAY

The Past and The Future were attending a lecture by Progress while their teenage babysitter (their next-door neighbour's child) looked after their two children. Once the children were safely tucked in, the babysitter stole The Past and The Future's weed and screwed her lover on their unmade bed.

The Past had been crying more than usual, and The Future was starting to pull away by focusing more on work and video games. The Past had seen an ad for the lecture at the public library and asked The Future if they should go. Despite not being particularly interested in the subject because they pretty much took Progress for granted, The Future agreed to go in hopes that The Past would be up for a drink or two and a tumble in the hay.

Before the event started, The Past squeezed The Future's hand in anticipation and said, —We really have to start getting out more often. We need to have more time for us. The Future nodded, all the while thinking about what The Past was wearing under their clothes and the night that lay ahead. When the lights dimmed and the introduction began, The Future started to nod off. Annoyed, The Past jabbed The Future in the ribs and The Future quickly sat up. No matter what, The Future did not want this night to end in a fight or tears.

But once Progress took the stage, there wasn't a sleepy eye in the place. Progress coughed and took a sip of water, then scanned the room, taking in all the eager and hopeful faces. —I wish I came bearing good news, Progress said with a little smile. —But the truth is that by the time my work is over, your life as you have known it will be worth less than a pile of dust, and your children's lives will be worth less than that. And their children's lives, well, what more can I say?

Raising a shaky hand in the quiet, still auditorium, The Past said in a voice louder than anyone expected, —But that's not the story we've always been told.

—Exactly, Progress said. —Next question.

THE SWAP

The Past and The Future decided to swap lives like in that movie *The Parent Trap* to see if things might turn out differently.

The Future put on The Past's hat and vice versa.

The first thing The Past did as The Future was to get an ice-cream cone from an ice-cream truck and then walk to the swimming pool instead of running.

The Future, however, took things a little more seriously. When The Past wasn't paying attention and was splashing around in the kiddie pool with all their new friends, The Future came up behind them and smashed in The Past's skull with a baseball bat. It exploded like a watermelon.

The onlookers stared at The Future (who they thought was The Past) with their mouths hanging open. Everyone stayed still, afraid to move, afraid of what The Future would do next.

—Don't worry, everybody. I'm not going do anything to anyone else. Trust me, The Future said with a crooked smile, and pointed at The Past. —I was after them, not you.

SUNSET

One evening The Future walked down to the boardwalk to look out at the ocean.

A young man was standing on the sand by the shore, holding up a tripod and filming himself talking into his phone. He sounded like he had memorized some kind of a script for an instructional video.

A family with a black Lab walked past the man on the beach. They were throwing a stick into the ocean, and the dog dove in to retrieve it. The man with the tripod was annoyed and walked in the opposite direction from the family. When he was far enough away, he began recording himself again.

The Past stepped onto the boardwalk and approached The Future with great excitement. —You should've seen that dog. He couldn't wait to get off his leash. And when they took it off, he just beelined into the ocean.

They watched the dog play in the water, and then The Future said, —Not a bad life.

The Past sighed. —It's a short one.

The Future nodded, and then The Past said, —Well, these days maybe that's not such a bad thing.

—Yeah, The Future said.

—We're heading in such a wrong direction, said The Past.

The Future couldn't agree more and was grateful The Past had the courage to say it.

Together they watched the dog until the sun went down, then they bid each other a good evening before heading home.

BETTER

—Things always get better, don't they? The Future said to The Past, who was fast asleep.

It didn't matter.

It was partly a question The Future was posing to the universe and partly a way to cheer themselves along.

ACKNOWLEDGEMENTS

Thanks to Hazel Millar and Jay MillAr and everyone at Book*hug Press for making this book possible and bringing so much excellent writing into the world. I'm honoured to have my book among such works.

Malcolm Sutton is a writer and editor I've long admired. I'm deeply indebted to Malcolm for his sharp editorial eye and patience throughout the editorial process. This was no small task. I wish for every writer to have the care of such an editor. And thank you, Malcolm, for the cover illustration and design of *Anecdotes*. Words cannot express how much I adore it!

For me, writing exists in community with other writers.

I'd like to thank Gary Barwin for his friendship and collaboration. Earlier versions of "It's Anticipation That's Keeping Me Alive," "Cookies," "When a Tree Develops Problems," "Whitecaps," and "Psychics" were drafted during back-and-forth collaborative writing in 2017.

Early drafts of "Hard to Get" and "Fuck Truck" were drafted during back-and-forth collaborative writing with my dear friend Hoang Pham in 2022.

I'd like to thank readers and supporters of my newsletter *Send My Love to Anyone*, where I have written about the writing process and the process of writing this book.

Thanks to the *Watch Your Head* editorial collective and the contributors who share their work on the climate crisis, inspiring me to share mine; to my students and colleagues in the Writing Department at the University of Victoria; and to my former students and colleagues at Western University.

I'm grateful to my friends Kirby, Tom Prime, and Danielle Geller for our many writing conversations; to my oldest and dearest friend Eleni Kapetanios; and to my family—my in-laws Judy and Len Hicken, my sister Susan Mockler, and my mother Joyce Mockler—for their love and support.

This book would not exist without my husband and first reader, David Poolman, who I am so grateful to have in my life.

Anecdotes was supported by the Canada Council and the Ontario Arts Council Recommender Program.

Excerpts of "This Isn't a Conversation" have been adapted into short experimental videos and have screened at international film and video festivals.

Early versions of these stories previously appeared in the following publications. Thanks to the editors of these magazines and journals for publishing this work. "When a Tree Develops Problems," *Windsor Review*, vol. 54, no. 2, March 2022; "This Isn't a Conversation" (previously titled "Let's Say"), Micro-climate Stories, Guelph Institute for Environmental Research, online, 2021; "Tumble in the Hay" and "Dark Thoughts," *Fence Magazine*, Winter 2021; "Birds," *Me Then You Then Me Then*, a collaboration with Gary Barwin, published by knife | fork | book, 2020; "I Won't Clean the Tub," *Geist Magazine*, Issue 109, 2018; "My Dream House" (previously titled "The Dream House"), "The Sunburn," "The Bed," "The Swap," and "Let's Play Oil Slick," *Some Theories*, by Kathryn Mockler and David Poolman (illustrator), 2018; "The People Skirt," *Chicago Review*, #METOO, 2018; "I Shit Here," "Date Night," and "The Swap," *Dreamland*, February 2017; "Two Friends on a Beach" (previously titled "Two Women on a Beach"), *Entropy Magazine*, May 10, 2017; "The Job Interview: A Murder," *Danforth Review*, September 10, 2017; "A Laugh," *Minola Review*, Issue 5, July 31, 2016; "Sit Down Beside Megan," *Cosmonauts Avenue*, 2nd Anniversary Issue, November 15, 2016; "The Boy Is Dead," *The Butter*, May 8, 2015; "Freight," *Found Press*, Spring 2015; "My Dream House" (previously titled "The Dream House"), *Poetry Is Dead*, F/U/T/U/R/E, Issue 10, November 2014; "Remote Control," *Vol. 1 Brooklyn*, November 30, 2014.

NOTES

"When a Tree Develops Problems"—Some lines borrowed from this article: https://extension.umd.edu/resource/how-do-you-decide-when-remove-tree

The line "If I Die, Will You Die?" in "How Can You Go On?" is from an SNFU song, "If I Die, Will You Die?"

ABOUT THE AUTHOR

KATHRYN MOCKLER is the author of five books of poetry. She co-edited the print anthology *Watch Your Head: Writers and Artists Respond to the Climate Crisis* (2020) and is the publisher of the Watch Your Head website. She runs *Send My Love to Anyone*, a literary newsletter, and is an assistant professor at the University of Victoria, where she teaches screenwriting and fiction.

Colophon

Manufactured as the first edition of
Anecdotes
in the fall of 2023 by Book*hug Press

Edited for the press by Malcolm Sutton
Copy edited by Stuart Ross
Proofread by Charlene Chow
Type + design by Malcolm Sutton

Printed in Canada

bookhugpress.ca